# THE BALL OF SNOW

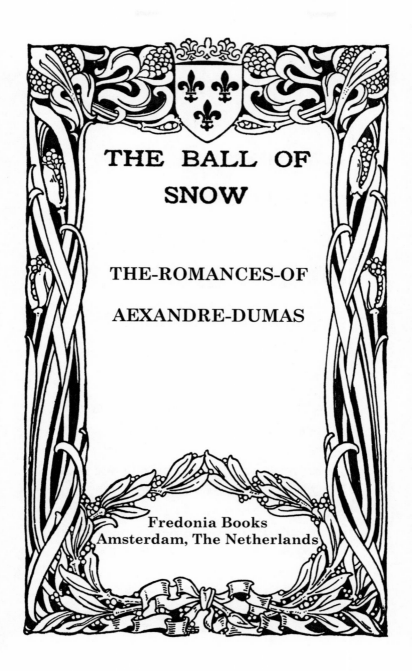

# THE BALL OF SNOW

## THE-ROMANCES-OF

## AEXANDRE-DUMAS

Fredonia Books
Amsterdam, The Netherlands

The Ball of Snow

by
Alexandre Dumas

ISBN: 1-58963-755-0

Reprinted from the 1895 edition

Fredonia Books
Amsterdam, the Netherlands
http://www.fredoniabooks.com

# INTRODUCTORY NOTE.

FROM fresh fields and pastures new, Dumas gathered the material of the two romances of this volume. The scenes and characters of " The Ball of Snow " are as vividly Oriental as those of his French novels are French, and yet they possess a keen, next-door-neighborly savor, such as could be developed only by passing through the alembic of his brain. The precision with which Dumas lays his finger on the kindred touches of nature is his greatest charm. That East is West is no paradox to him.

In " Sultanetta " Dumas evidently struggled against assimilating the story of the Russian novelist whose romance he admits, under a somewhat specious plea, that he " re-wrote." His pen rebelled against another's tactics, and oftener than not became a free lance.

In giving these two tales of the Caucasus to the readers of English only, the translator enjoys the delights of an approving conscience, properly tempered, however, by the cold douche administered to all trans-lators, — " *i traditori traduttori.*"

ALMA BLAKEMAN JONES

SIERRA MADRE. CALIFORNIA.

# LIST OF CHARACTERS.

## THE BALL OF SNOW.

### Period, 1830.

HADJI FESTAHLI, a holy Mussulman.
KASSIME, his niece.
KITCHINA, friend to Kassime.
ISKANDER BEG, a young Tartar in love with Kassime
YUSSEF, his friend.
HUSSEIN } inhabitants of Derbend.
FERZALI }
DJAFFAR, a goldsmith.
MULLAH SÉDEK, friend of Hadji Festahli.
MONZARAM BEG, chief of police at Derbend.
MULLAH NOUR, a brigand.
GOULCHADE, his wife.

# CONTENTS.

## THE BALL OF SNOW.

# THE BALL OF SNOW.

## I.

### FORTY DEGREES IN THE SHADE.[1]

The sad, sonorous voice of the muëzzin was heard as a dirge for the brilliant May day that was just sweeping into eternity.

"Allah! it is hot weather for Derbend! Go up on the roof, Kassime, and see how the sun is setting behind the mountain. Is the west red? Are there clouds in the sky?"

"No, uncle; the west is as blue as the eyes of Kitchina; the sun is setting in all its glory; it looks like a flaming rose upon the breast of evening, and the last ray that falls upon the earth has not to pierce the slightest fog."

Night has unfurled her starry fan; the shadows have fallen.

"Go up on the roof, Kassime," bade the same voice, 'and see if the dew is not dripping from the rim of the moon. Is she not lurking in a misty halo, like a pearl in its brilliant shell?"

[1] 1° Réaumur is equivalent to 2¼° Fahrenheit. — Tr.

"No, uncle; the moon is floating in an azure ocean; she is pouring her burning beams into the sea. The roofs are as dry as the steppes of the Mogan, and the scorpions are playing about gayly."

"Ah," said the old man, with a sigh, "it means that to-morrow will be as warm as to-day. The best thing to do, Kassime, is to go to bed."

And the old man falls asleep, dreaming of his silver; and his niece falls asleep dreaming of what a young girl of sixteen always dreams, whatever her nationality may be, — of love; and the town falls asleep dreaming that it was Alexander the Great who had built the Caucasian Wall and forged the iron gates of Derbend.

And so, toward midnight, everything slept.

The only sounds to be heard, in the general stillness, were the warnings of the sentinels to each other, "*Slouchay!*" (watch!) and the moaning of the Caspian sea, as it advanced to press its humid lips upon the burning sands of the shore.

One could have fancied the souls of the dead to be communing with eternity, and this conception would have been the more striking, since nothing so resembles a vast cemetery as the city of Derbend.

Long before day the surface of the sea seemed ablaze. The swallows, awake before the muézzin, were singing upon the mosque.

True, they did not much precede him. The sounds of his footsteps put them to flight. He advanced upon the minaret, bowing his head upon his hand, and crying out in measured tones that lent his words the effect, if not the form, of a chant, —

"Awake ye, arise, Mussulmans; prayer is better than sleep!"

One voice answered his: it said. —

"Go up on the roof, Kassime, and see if a mist is not descending from the mountains of Lesghistan. Tell me, is not the sea obscured?"

"No, uncle; the mountains seem covered with pure gold; the sea shines like a mirror; the flag above the fortress of Nazinkale hangs in folds along its staff like a veil about a young girl's form. The sea is still; not the slightest puff of wind lifts an atom of dust from the highway; all is calm on the earth, all serene in the sky."

The face of the old man became gloomy, and, after performing his ablutions, he went up on the roof to pray.

He unfolded the prayer-rug that he carried under his arm and knelt upon it, and, when he had finished his prayer by rote, he began to pray from the heart.

"*Bismillahir rahmanir rahim!*" he cried, looking sadly about him.

Which means, —

"May my voice resound to the glory of the holy and merciful God!"

Then he proceeded to say in Tartar what we shall say in French, at the risk of divesting the prayer of Kassime's uncle of the picturesque character imparted to it by the language of Turkestan.

"O clouds of spring-time, children of our world, why do ye linger on the rocky heights? why hide ye in caves, like Lesghian brigands. Ye like to rove about the mountains, and sleep upon the snowy peaks of granite. Be it so; but could ye not find yourselves better amusement than pumping all the humidity from our plains, only to turn it upon forests that are impenetrable to man and permit to descend into our valleys naught but cataracts of flint that look like the dried bones of your victims, ye capricious children of the air?

See how our unhappy earth opens a thousand mouths! She is parched with thirst; she implores a little rain. See how the wheat-blades shrink; how they break when a butterfly imprudently lights upon them; how they lift their heads, hoping to inhale a little freshness, and are met by the sun's rays, which lap them like flame. The wells are dry; the flowers hold no perfume; the leaves on the trees shrivel and fall; the grass dries up; the madder is lost, the crickets grow hoarse, the death-rattle of the cicada is heard, the buffaloes fight for a streamlet of mud; the children dispute over a few drops of water. O God! O God! what is to become of us? Drouth is the mother of famine; famine is the mother of pestilence; pestilence is the twin of robbery!    O cool wind of the mountains, waft hither on your wings the blessing of Allah! Ye clouds, life-giving bosoms, pour the milk of heaven down upon the land!    Whirl into storms, if ye will, but refresh the earth!    Strike down the wicked with your thunderbolts, if ye deem it best, but spare the innocent!    Gray clouds, wings of the angels, bring us moisture; come, hasten, fly!    Speed ye, and ye shall have welcome."

But the old Tartar prays in vain, the clouds are invisible.    It is sultry, it is stifling, and the inhabitants of Derbend are quite prepared to seek for coolness in their ovens.

And note well that this was the month of May, just when St. Petersburg hears a loud crashing at the northeast as the ice of the Ladoga breaks up and threatens to sweep away the bridges of the Neva; when a man catches cold while crossing the Place d'Isaac; when he gets inflammation of the chest by turning the corner of the Winter Palace; when people shout at each other, from Smolnyi to the English embankment, —

" You are going out ? Don't forget your cloaks! "

At St. Petersburg they were thinking of the spring, which was, perhaps, approaching; at Derbend they took thought of the harvesting, which was almost at hand.

For five weeks, not a drop of rain had fallen in South Daghestan, and it would have been forty degrees in the shade if there had been any shade in Derbend. As a fact, it was fifty-two degrees in the sun.

A drouth in the Orient is a terrible thing. It scorches the fields and deprives every living creature of nourishment, — the birds of the air, the beasts of the field, the dwellers in cities. In a country where the transportation of grain is always difficult, often impossible, drouth is invariably the forerunner of famine. An Asiatic lives from day to day, forgetful of yesterday, unmindful of to-morrow. He lives thus because ease and *far niente* are his dearest enjoyments; but when there is no Joseph to interpret the parable of the seven lean kine, when misfortune falls suddenly upon his shoulders in the hideous guise of famine, when to-morrow becomes to-day, he begins to complain that he is not granted the means of living. Instead of seeking them, he waxes wroth, and, when he should act, his cowardice augments the evil, as his incredulity has abridged it.

You can now judge of the trouble they were in at Derbend, a city wholly Tartar, and, consequently, wholly Asiatic, when this desert heat began to destroy the prospects of both merchants and husbandmen.

To tell the truth, at that time Daghestan had many reasons for anxiety; the fanatical Kasi Mullah, the adoptive father of Schamyl, was at the height of his fame; the inhabitants of Daghestan had revolted, and more bullets had been sown in their fields than wheat; fire had destroyed the houses, whose ashes the sun kept hot; and the mountaineers, instead of harvesting, rode under the standard of Kasi Mullah or hid themselves in caves and forests to escape the Russians, or, rather, to fall upon their backs when they were least on guard.

The result was not difficult to foretell, — it was famine. The sowing not having been done, the harvest was wanting. Anything that the war had spared — silver plate, rich arms, beautiful carpets — was sold for a mere trifle at the bazaar. The most beautiful necklace of pearls in Derbend could have been bought with a sack of flour.

The man possessed of neither plate, nor arms, nor tapestries, nor pearls, began upon his flocks, eating such as had been left him by friend and foe, or Russian and mountaineer. The poor began to come down from the mountains and beg for alms in the city, while waiting until they could take without asking.

At last, vessels loaded with flour arrived from Astrakhan. Through pity or fear, the rich helped the poor; the people were quieted for a time.

The new harvest could yet right matters.

The fête of the Khatil had come, and it had been celebrated by the inhabitants of Derbend.

The Khatil is a religious festival in memory of the fate of Shah Hussein, the first caliph, a martyr of the sect of Ali. They made merry while it lasted, with the childish gayety of the Orientals.

Thanks to this fête, the only diversion of the people during the entire year, they had gradually forgotten the crops and the heat, or, rather, they had forgotten nothing; no, they had in all simplicity thanked Heaven that the rain had not interfered with their pleasures. But, when the fête was over, when they found themselves face to face with the reality, when they awoke with parched mouths, when they saw their fields baked by the sun, they lost their heads.

It was interesting then to note the wagging of red beards and black, to mark the rattling of beads as they slipped through the fingers.

Every face was long, and only repinings were heard.

It was really no laughing matter to lose a crop, and have to pay two roubles a measure for flour without knowing what must be paid for it later.

The poor trembled for their lives, the rich for their purses. Stomachs and pockets crept close together at the mere thought of it.

Then it was that the Mussulmans began to pray in the mosque.

The rain came not.

They prayed in the fields, thinking that in the open air they stood two chances to one, — the one of being seen, the other of being heard.

Not a drop of water fell.

What was to be done?

They fell back on their magi.

First, the boys spread their handkerchiefs in the middle of the streets and collected the coins that were thrown into them. Purchasing wax tapers and rose-water, and fastening tree branches to the body of the most beautiful boy, they decked him with flowers and covered him with ribbons, and then followed him in a procession through the streets, chanting verses to Goudoul, the god of rain.

The hymn ended with a strophe of thanksgiving. They did not doubt that Goudoul would answer the prayers of his worshippers.

Thus, for three days, the young boys shouted at the tops of their voices this thanksgiving, which we trans

late, without any pretension of rendering otherwise
than very feebly the Arabic poem: —

> " Goudoul, Goudoul, O god of rain,
> The drouth has fled from mount and plain;
> Thy voice from heaven the rain doth send.
> Then go, fair maid, unto the rill!
> And high thy jar with water fill,
> Till thou beneath its weight doth bend."

And all the youths of Derbend danced around the
beribboned and garlanded Tartar, so sure of rain that,
as we see, they were sending the young girls in advance
to the fountain.

And, in truth, clouds gathered in the sky; the sun
sulked like a miser obliged to surrender the treasure
that had been intrusted to him. The city took on the
dreary look that dull weather imparts.

But the darker the sky became, the greater was the
people's joy.

A few drops of rain fell.

They cried out with fervor, —

" *Sekour Allah!* "

But their joy was short-lived; the wind blew up
from Persia as hot as if it had come from a furnace, and
drove away the very last remnant of a cloud, which
betook itself to St. Petersburg to fall as snow. The
sun glared worse than ever; the grass crumbled under
the heat; the flowers bent their heads, and the faithful
began to doubt, not Mahomet's might, but Goudoul's.

Another day dawned; the sun pursued his blazing
path, then he sank behind the mountain, like a weary
traveller in the burning sands of the desert.

On that night and the next morning the two conversations which opened this chapter took place between
Kassime and her uncle.

The old Tartar had then addressed to the clouds the prayer that we have attempted to translate.    But, in spite of his fervent prayer, that day, like the preceding one, passed without a drop of rain.

And on that day the commander of Derbend announced that the thermometer had registered forty-two degrees in the shade and fifty-two degrees in the sun.

## II.

### A HOLY MUSSULMAN.

AH! when you go to Derbend, traveller, from whatever country you hail, — whether you come from the
south, the north, the east or the west, — go, I entreat
you, to see the principal mosque.

Otherwise, as the Catholics say, you will have been
to Rome without seeing the pope.

What would you have to relate about Derbend, I ask,
if you had not seen the great mosque?

While, if you have seen it, it is a very different
matter.

"The great mosque," you say, snapping your snuff-
box, or flicking the ashes from your cigar, if you are
only a smoker, "the mosque," you say, "was formerly
a Christian church — "

Proceed boldly, I assume all responsibility.

" It was a church, a Christian church, rather, because
its face is turned to the east, while the Mussulman
mosques of the northern Orient should veer southerly,
in nautical phrase, in order to look toward the two holy
cities, — Mecca, where the prophet was born; Medina,
where he was buried."

This gives you at the outset a somewhat learned air
which sits well.   Proceed.

" Upon entering, you discover a great court shaded
by magnificent plane-trees, with a well in the centre

Three doors, always open, symbolically and practically summon the Mussulmans to prayer.

" A verse from the Koran inscribed over the principal door attracts the attention. Enter: but first put off the shoes from your feet; put away earthly thoughts from your mind. Into the house of Allah bring not the clay of the street, nor of the mind. Fall upon your knees and lift up your prayer. Reckon not your rents, but your sins. *La illah il Allah! Mohammed rassoul Allah!* — that is to say: There is no God but God, and Mahomet is his prophet."

Here you cough and make a pause; that was quite worth the trouble. You have an air of knowing Turk.

You resume: —

" Mussulmans are long at their prayers, remaining on their knees or prostrate on the prayer-rug, as they pass from adoration to ecstasy, and nothing, especially in this last state, can then distract their attention."

Memory then reverts to the past, and you exclaim, —

" Where are you, Christian builders of this temple? are you now remembered anywhere but in heaven? You are forgotten, even in the history of Derbend, and the words of the Koran echo to-day where formerly sounded the hymns of the prophet king."

And now that you have given your account, now that you have acquired the right to be a corresponding member of the section of inscriptions and *belles-lettres* of the French Academy, the most learned, as you know, of all academies, I again take up the thread of my history; for this, pray take note, is history.

I resume then, the thread of my history.

Among Mussulmans of all countries, and particularly among the Mussulmans of Daghestan, the court of the mosque is the usual place of meeting. There the mer-

chants gather to talk over their commercial interests, and
the Tartar chiefs, their political issues.   The first have
but one aim, — to get the better of their customers; the
second, but one hope, — to throw off the yoke of their
master.   The former have vowed to Allah to be honest;
the latter have sworn to the emperor to be faithful.
But, in Asia, oddly enough, — and this will astonish
our public officers, our judges and senators, — the oath
is regarded as a simple formality, of no consequence and
not binding.

Does this, perchance, mean that the Asiatics, whom
we believe to be behind us in the matter of civilization,
are, on the contrary, in advance?

This would be very humiliating, and, in such case,
we must hasten to overtake them.

You must know that at this period of frightful heat,
which we have tried to depict, the court of the mosque
— the only place where there were any trees, consequently any shade, consequently only forty degrees of
heat — was full of people.   Effendis with white beards,
muftis with red, were talking in the centre of circles
more or less wide, according as they were more or less
eloquent; but the learning of these and the dignity of
those did not cause the sky to sweat the least drop of
moisture, and the beards of all lengths and of all colors
were powerless even to invent an equivalent.   They
talked much, they argued still more; but at last discourse and discussion ended this way: —

" *Nedgeleikh?*   (What shall we do now?) "

Shoulders went up to the ears, eyebrows to the
papaks; many voices in many keys united in one
cry, —

" *Amani! amani!*   (Spare us! spare us!) "

Finally, a prince began to speak.

He was not only a prince, but a saint, — a combination which was formerly seen in Russia and France, but which is to be met with to-day only in the Orient.

It is true that his saintship, like his principality, came to him by inheritance; he was related in the sixty-second degree to Mahomet, and, as we know, all relatives of Mahomet, of whatsoever degree, are saints.

His eloquence grew heated in the smoke of his kabam, and golden speech emanated from the fumes of the Turkish tobacco.

" '*Amani! amani!*' you cry to Allah; and think you that, for this one word, Allah will be so simple as to pardon you and put faith in your repentance without other proof? No! kiss not the Koran with lips still smeared with the fat of pork; no, you do not deceive God with your flatteries and plaintive tones. He is not a Russian governor; he has known you this long while. Your hearts are covered with more stains than there are sins in the book in which the angel Djebrael records the faults of men! Do not think to cleanse your hearts from one day to the next by prayer and fasting. God beholds your image in the sunlight of day and the starlight of night; he knows every thought of your mind, every impulse of your heart; he knows how you go to the pharmacies, and, on a pretext of buying balsam, manage to get brandy under a false label. But God is not to be deceived by such means. The word of Mahomet is decisive: ' He who in this world has drunk the juice of the vine, in the other shall not drink the wine of gladness.' No! you will have no rain for your crops, because you have drained the source of the rains of heaven by exhausting the patience of the Lord! Allah is great, and you are yourselves the cause of your misery."

The orator ceased speaking, raised his eyes toward
the heavens, grasped his beard with his hand; and, in
this attitude, he was not unlike Jupiter about to hurl
from his mighty hand a sheaf of thunderbolts.

And, sooth to say, a very eminent scholar was Mir
Hadji Festahli Ismael Ogli. From the beginning of his
speech it was as if one were listening to a brooklet's
murmuring or a nightingale's singing. Every word
produced upon the by-standers the effect of a melting
pastel, and there was not, in all Daghestan, a single
effendi who understood the half of what he was saying.
The interpreter of the commander of Derbend himself,
Mirza Aly, who had swallowed, digested, and thrown
up criticisms upon all the poets of Farzistan, after having talked with him for more than two hours, ended by
saying, —

"I can make nothing of it."

This, in Tartar, corresponds to the Russian saying,
which, I think, is also a little French: "I throw my
tongue to the dogs."

This time our orator had taken the trouble to make
himself clear, so that he had been understood by everybody, as was expedient in a conjuncture of such importance; hence his discourse had produced the greatest
effect. They gathered around him with mingled respect
and awe, and these words were heard murmured on all
sides: "He is right, he speaks the truth;" and each
man, like a bee, regaled him with the honey of praise.

Thereupon, addressing himself anew to his auditors,
with the confidence gained from his first success, he
said, —

"Listen, brethren; we are all guilty in the eyes of
Allah, and I stand quite the first; our faults have
mounted to the third heaven, but, happily, there are

seven of them, and four remain to us in which to seek for God's mercy. He punishes the innocent with the guilty; yet, sometimes, for a single good man, he saves a whole people. Well, I am going to make you a proposition. Whether you will accept it or not, I do not know, but here it is: This is not the first time that Daghestan has prayed for water; well, our fathers and grandfathers, who were wiser than we, were accustomed, under such circumstances, to chose from among the young Mussulmans a youth pure in mind and body, and send him, with the prayers and blessings of all, up to the summit of the mountain nearest to Allah, — that is, to the top of Schach Dagh. There he must pray fervently, as one who prays for a whole people; he must take some unsullied snow from the mountain, make a ball of the size of his head, enclose it in a vase, and then, without permitting it to touch the earth, he must bring it to Derbend. Finally, at Derbend he must turn the melted snow into the sea. God is great. The snow-water from Schach Dagh will scarcely have mingled with the waters of the Caspian sea before the clouds are heaped above the mingled waters, and the down-pouring rain refreshes the parched earth."

" It is true! it is true! " cried every voice.

" I have heard my father tell about it," said one.

" And I my grandfather," said another.

" And I have seen it," said, as he advanced, an old man with a white beard whose extremity alone was tinged with red.

They turned and listened to him.

" It was my brother," continued the old man, " that went to get the ball of snow; the miracle was performed; the waters of the Caspian sea became as fresh as milk; the raindrops were as large as silver roubles; never,

in the memory of man, had there been so fine a harvest
as that year's."

The old man was silent.

Then there was but one cry.

They must choose a messenger, must pick him out that
very instant, must send him to Schach Dagh without
losing a moment.

" To Schach Dagh! to Schach Dagh!" they shouted.

As by a train of gunpowder, the words reached the
town, and all Derbend cried with one voice, like an
echo of the mosque, —

" To Schach Dagh! to Schach Dagh!"

The solution of the great puzzle was therefore discovered; they knew then at last a sure way to bring
rain.    Everybody danced with delight and screamed for
joy.

The rich especially appeared enchanted that a means
had been found that would not cost a kopeck.

There is no one like a rich man for appreciating
economical measures.

The young men said proudly, —

" They will choose from among us; upon one of us
depends the fate of Daghestan."

But where was this young man to be found, pure of
body and mind?   In any nation it would be difficult;
but among the Asiatics! —

While reflecting upon this question, the inhabitants
of Derbend were much embarrassed, and the efferves-
cence of their first exultation subsided.

Where, indeed, was this innocent young man to be
found who knew as yet neither the savor of wine nor
the sweetness of a kiss?

They began to consider the matter seriously, to point
out this one, then that one; but the one was too young,

the other too experienced.    The first had as yet no
moustache; that of the second was too long.    It was a
dreadful affair to manage successfully.

What we have just·said is not entirely to the credit of
the inhabitants of Derbend; but, I repeat, this is history
that I am writing: truth, then, before everything.

If this were a romance!   Ah!   *pardieu!*  my hero
would already be found.

" We must take Sopharkouli," said some; " he is as
shy as a young girl. "

So shy that, afraid of no one knows what, he had
been seen, three days before, to leap, at peep o' day,
from his fair neighbor's terrace into the street, enter
hastily his own house, and lock his door with a double
turn.

" Or Mourad Annet; he leads a life as quiet and
solitary as a lily. "

But it was affirmed that a month before, upon returning home with a bottle of balsam in each hand, after a
visit to the pharmacy, the immaculate lily had sung
songs that would have made the devils themselves clap
their hands to their ears.

There still remained Mohammed Rassoul; surely no
one could speak evil of him.    However, they might
think it.    He had in his house a charming Lesghienne
whom he had bought from her father; he had paid only
twenty-nine roubles, and had since refused a hundred
for her.    He was a man after all; a sword of steel sometimes rusts.

They sought in vain; too much was said of this one;
that one said too much of himself.

Melancholy began to possess the inhabitants of Derbend, and under such circumstances there is but a step
from melancholy to despair.

2

" And Iskander Beg ? " said a voice in the crowd.

" Iskander Beg, surely! Excellent! Iskander Beg!
Ferfect! How did we forget Iskander Beg? It is
incredible! incomprehensible! As well overlook a rose
in a bouquet, a pomegranate in a dish of fruit! Allah!
Allah! The heat has shrivelled up our wits. "

" Well," said a voice, " Allah be praised! we have
found our man! Call Iskander Beg! "

" Iskander Beg! Iskander Beg, hallo! Iskander
Beg, hallo! "

" Now indeed are we saved," was declared on all sides.
" This dear Iskander Beg! this excellent Iskander Beg!
this noble Iskander Beg! Why, he scarcely eats! he
never drinks! *He* is not hand-in-glove with unbelievers. No one remembers having ever met him in
a garden. Who has ever seen him look at a woman?
Have you? "

" No."

" Or you ? "

" Nor I, either. He lives apart like the moon."

" Well, then, let us run to Iskander Beg's house! "
cried several voices.

" But people don't go to Iskander Beg's like that."

" Why ? "

" Because he is so dignified that a man does not know
how to approach him; so haughty that one speaks only
when spoken to; so sparing of speech that one would
say every word cost him a rouble. Who ever saw him
laugh, hey ? "

" Not I."

" Nor I."

" Nor I. We must think twice about it before going
to his house."

" There is but one man that might venture to run the
risk." said a voice.

And every one answered, —

"That man is Mir Hadji Festahli Ismael Ogli."

It was indeed very proper that the one who had given the advice should finish what he had begun.

"Go, Hadji Festahli, go," cried the by-standers, "and entreat Iskander in the name of us all! Get his consent; you will have no difficulty, you are so eloquent!"

Hadji Festahli was not eager for the honor; but, in the end, he agreed to undertake the commission. They gave him two begs as escort, — the fat Hussein and the lean Ferzali.

The deputation set out.

"Ah!" said the crowd, "that is well."

"I am as tranquil now," said one, "as if Iskander had accepted."

"If Festahli has a mind, he is sure to succeed," said another.

"He could coax half a beard away from a poor man."

"He is cleverer than the devil."

"A very respectable man!"

"He is a genius!"

"He could make a serpent dance on its tail."

"And what eloquence! when he speaks, they are not mere words that fall from his mouth — "

"They are flowers!"

"The ears have not even time to gather them in."

"He could so cheat you that he could get judgment against you for having been taken in by him."

"But we could not have sent him for the ball of snow."

"He is not chaste enough for that."

"Nor sober enough."

"Nor brave enough."

" Nor quite — "

Permit us to break off from the eulogies of Mir Hadji
Festahli.   We are not of those who, after bathing a
man's eyes with rose-water, — as the Tartars say, —
give him, while he is drying them, a scorpion instead
of a cherry to eat, or an aconite blossom in place of a
jasmine to smell.

## III.

### ISKANDER BEG.

THE respectable Hadji Festahli proceeded slowly as he climbed the ladder of streets that leads to the higher part of the city, in which stood the house of Iskander Beg. From time to time he had to pass through streets so narrow that his two honorable companions, Hussein and Ferzali, who walked beside him along the streets where they could go three abreast, were then obliged to fall back and walk behind him in single file, — a humiliation from which they made haste to escape as soon as the street became wide enough for three abreast. Occasionally one or the other would attempt to engage the hadji in conversation; but so great was his pre-occupation, he did not hear them, did not answer; and he was even so absent-minded that he failed to observe that in spitting to right and left, he sometimes spat upon the black beard of Hussein, sometimes upon the red beard of Ferzali.

His inattention continued so long that his two companions began to be angry.

"This is a singular man!" said Hussein; "he is spoken to, and, instead of replying, he spits."

"May it fall into his throat!" cried Ferzali, wiping his beard. "The proverb says truly, Hussein: 'If the master is at home, it is sufficient to speak his name, and the door will be opened to you; but if he is not there, you will get nothing, even by breaking in.'

Useless to speak any more to Mir Hadji Festahli; his mind is elsewhere, the house is empty."

Ferzali *à la barbe rose*, as they called him in Derbend, because, instead of employing the two substances in use among the Tartars for coloring the beard, — substances, the first of which begins by tinting the beard red, and the second finishes by dyeing it black, — Ferzali, who used only the first, and who, consequently, kept his beard the color of the first streak of dawn as it appears on the verge of the horizon — Ferzali was deceived. The house was not empty; it was, on the contrary, so full of its own occupants, and their strife was creating such an uproar, that, not being able to understand even the voice of his own mind, Hadji Festahli could not understand other people's voices.

This was what his thoughts were urging: " Have a care, Festahli! every step that you take toward the dwelling of Iskander Beg brings you nearer to danger. Remember how seriously you have offended him. Beware, Hadji Festahli, beware! "

What, then, had passed between Hadji Festahli and Iskander Beg?

We are about to relate it.

Iskander was born at Derbend, when the city was already occupied by the Russians, — this occupation dates from 1795; but his father had been the intimate friend of the last khan, who had been driven from his provinces by Catherine's army. In 1826, he died of chagrin because the Persians, whom he was expecting at Derbend, had been routed at Kouba, to which point they had advanced; but, when dying, he had charged his son, then fifteen years of age, never to serve the Russians, and never to make friends with the inhabitants of Derbend, who had repelled the Persians.

He was dead; but his convictions, his habits, his opinions, all survived in his son, whose ideas, thoughts, and desires were all opposed to the desires, thoughts, and ideas of the inhabitants of Derbend. A handful of rice, a glass of water, a little light, much air, were all of which the young Iskander Beg had need.

In the spring, when the entire world was awakening to the breath of love and poetry, he would saddle his good Karabach horse, swing from his shoulder the fine gun from Hadji Moustaff, the most celebrated gunsmith in Daghestan, and, with his bold yellow falcon perched upon his thumb, he would hunt the pheasant over mountain and valley until he was ready to drop with fatigue, if you grant there can be fatigue in the pursuit of a passion. Then he would dismount from his horse, which he allowed to wander at will, lie down in the shade of some great tree beside a stream, and sleep tranquilly to its gentle sound. Whether its sweet harmony caused him to dream, whether his dreams were prosaic, whether he was poet or philosopher, rhymer or reasoner, I know not. This I do know, — he lived tingling with the thrill of life. What more would you have ?

In winter, when the snow, driven by the wind, beat against his windows, he loved to listen to the howling of the storm whirling over his chimney; stretched upon his rug, his eyes would follow the play of the embers upon his hearth, or the curling smoke from his pipe.

Did he see the figure of the devil in the embers ? Did he see angels' wings in the smoke from his pipe ? He said so, himself. The fact is, he dwelt in a nameless realm, and in this realm, of which he was king, he rummaged boxes of emeralds, pearls, and diamonds; he carried off women beside whom the houris, green, yellow,

and blue, promised by Mahomet to the faithful, were
but Kalmucks or Samoyedes; he cast himself into un-
heard of perils; he fought gnomes, giants, enchanters,
and fell asleep amidst the creatures of his fancy, and
awoke in the morning, the ideal so confused with the
real that he did not know whether he had been awake
or dreaming.

And sometimes he would summon his Lesghian noukar
and have him sing.   The Lesghian sang of the freedom
of his brothers upon their mountains, their courage in
combat and the chase; and then the Asiatic heart of
Iskander would begin to swell.   He would take his
dagger and feel its point; he would sharpen the blade
of his shaska, and mutter, —

"Shall I, then, never fight?"

His wish was not long in being realized; Kası
Mullah attacked Derbend.   It was a fine opportunity
for brave men to test their mettle.

Iskander Beg did not overlook it.

He sallied forth with the Tartars, mounted on his
fine Karabach charger, which knew neither rocks nor
abysses; and he was always at the front.   To join him,
yes, that might be possible; but to pass him, never.
He did not run, he flew like the eagle, despatching
death far and near, first with his gun, then, the discharged gun swung from his shoulder, with kandjiar on
high, hurling himself with savage shouts upon the
enemy.

One day there had been an engagement near Kouba,
and having dislodged the Russians from a vineyard, the
Tartars began, notwithstanding their success, to riot,
according to the Asiatic custom, with two heads lopped
off and fastened to a standard taken from the enemy.
The Russian troops had already re-entered the town,

but a young Russian officer and a few Tartars, among whom we find Iskander Beg, had halted near the fountain. Bullets and balls were whistling around them; the Russian officer was at the time drinking of the pure, limpid water. Lifting his head, he saw before him Iskander Beg in simple close tunic of white satin; his rolled-up sleeves revealed hands and arms reddened with blood to the elbow.

He was leaning upon his gun, his lips curled in scorn, his eyes flashing through tears, blazing with wrath.

"What is the matter, Iskander?" demanded the Russian. "It strikes me that you have acquitted yourself well of your share of the work, and have nothing to regret."

"Hearts of hares!" he muttered. "They march regularly enough when advancing, but in retreat, they are wild goats."

"Well, after all," said the young Russian, "the day seems to be ours."

"Of course it is ours; but we have left poor Ishmael over there."

"Ishmael?" demanded the officer. "Isn't that the handsome lad that came to me at the beginning of the fight and begged me to give him some cartridges?"

"Yes; he was the only one I loved in all Derbend; an angelic soul. He is lost!"

And he wiped away a single tear that trembled upon his eyelid and could not decide to fall.

"Is he captured?" inquired the Russian.

"He is dead!" answered Iskander. "Braver than a man, he had all the imprudence of a child. He wanted to pick a bunch of grapes, and he cleared the space separating him from the vines. He lost his head by

it.  Before my eyes, the Lesghians cut his throat.  I
could not help him; there were ten men to deal with.
I killed three of them, that was all I could do.  Just
now they are retreating; they are insulting his body,
the wretches!  Come," cried he, turning to three or
four Tartars who stood listening, " who of you still has
some love, fidelity, and courage in his soul ?  Let him
return with me to rescue the body of a comrade."

" I will go with you myself," announced the Russian
officer.

" Let us go," said two of the Tartars also.

And they four rushed upon the band of Lesghians,
who, not expecting this sudden attack, and believing
that these four men were followed by a much greater
number, retreated before them; and they advanced to the
boy's body, took it up, and bore it back to the town.

At her gate, the mother was waiting.  She threw
herself upon the decapitated body with heart-rending
shrieks and tears.

Iskander gazed at her, his eyebrows drawn together;
and now it was not a single tear that trembled alone
upon his eyelid, — there were streams of them coursing
down his cheeks like waters from a fountain.

A mother's despair melted this lion's heart.

" How unfortunate that you are not a Russian! " said
the officer, extending his hand.

" How fortunate that you are not a Tartar! " replied
Iskander, grasping the hand.

One thing is well known: the moustache, which is
an indication of approaching maturity, is likewise the
herald of love.

Iskander had not escaped the universal law.  Every
hair of his moustache had sprouted upon his lip at the
very instant that a desire had sprung up in his heart,

— desires vague as yet, inexplicable to himself, but, like orange boughs, bearing on the same branch both fruit and flowers. Why do women like the moustache so much? Because, the symbol of love, it springs from the same source, and crisps in the warmth of desire. What seeks the youth with head erect, humid eye, smiling face, and ruby lip under the budding moustache?

Neither honors nor fortune, — only a kiss.

A virgin moustache is a bridge thrown across two loving mouths; a moustache —

Let us leave the moustaches here, they are carrying us too far; then, too, why, with gray moustache, talk of black or blonde?

Besides, moustaches, of whatever color, lead me from my subject.

I return, then.

In the month of the preceding April, Iskander had, according to his custom, set out for the chase. The day was beautiful; it was a true spring holiday; it was warm without heat, fresh without humidity. Iskander plunged into the midst of an ocean of verdure and flowers. He had now, for several hours, been going from gorge to gorge, from mountain to mountain; he wanted something, he knew not what. For the first time the air seemed difficult to breathe, for the first time, his heart beat without cause; his unquiet breast fluttered like a woman's veil.

And, speaking of veils, let us note a fact.

When Iskander formerly passed through the streets of Derbend, he would never have cast a look toward a woman, had she been unveiled to her girdle; while, on the contrary, from the very day on which he was able to twist the ends of his little black moustache between his fingers, every nose-tip, every lip, every brown eye

or blue that he could catch a glimpse of through a peep-
hole in a veil, turned him hot and cold at once.  It is
a positive fact that he had never studied anatomy; well,
in spite of his ignorance, he could picture to himself a
woman from the toe of her slipper to the top of her
veil, not only without error but even without oversight,
merely from catching sight of a little silk-stockinged
foot in a velvet slipper under a kanaos trouser embroidered with gold or silver.

I will not tell you whether, on this occasion, his
hunt was successful; I will say only that the hunter
was very distrait, — so distrait that, instead of seeking
the lonely haunts where pheasant and partridge are wont
to hide, he turned his horse toward two or three hamlets
where he had absolutely no business.

But the day was fine, and, whether standing at their
gates, or sitting on the house-tops, he hoped to see one
of those pretty little contemporaneous animals that he
had reconstructed with as much precision as the learned
Cuvier had reconstructed a mastodon, an ichthyosaurus,
a pterodactyl, or any other antediluvian monster.

Unfortunately, he had to be content with the speci-
mens already known.  Women were at their gates,
women were on the terraces, but the Mohammedan
women, who sometimes put aside their veils for unbelievers, never lift them for their compatriots.  The
result was that the desires of Iskander Beg, not finding
a face upon which to fix themselves, were scattered to
the winds.

The young man became sad, drew a profound sigh,
threw the bridle on his horse's neck, and left him master
to go what way he would.

This is what travellers and lovers ought always to do
when they have an intelligent horse.

The horse knew a delightful road leading home; on this road, under some tall plane-trees, was a spring forming a pool, at which he was in the habit of slaking his thirst: he took this route.

Iskander Beg paid no attention as to what path his horse was taking.

Little it mattered to him; he was riding in a dream.

And along with him, on both sides of the road, stalked all sorts of phantoms; these were women, all veiled it is true, but their veils were so carelessly worn that not one of them prevented his seeing what should have been unseen.

Suddenly Iskander reined in his horse; his vision seemed turned into reality.

At the edge of the spring was hidden a girl of fifteen or sixteen years, more beautiful than he had ever dreamed a woman could be. With the pure water she was cooling her beautiful face, which the April sun had tinted like a rose; then she gazed at herself in the shimmering mirror, smiled, and took so much pleasure in seeing herself smile, that she saw nothing else, listening the while to the birds that sang above her head, and hearing only their songs, which seemed to say: " Gaze into the fountain, beautiful child! Never was flower so fresh as thou mirrored there before; never will flower so fresh as thou be mirrored after thee! "

They doubtless said it to her in verse; but I am obliged to tell it in prose, not knowing the rules of poetry in bird language.

And they were right, the feathered flatterers; it was hard to imagine flower fresher, purer, more beautiful than this one which appeared to have sprung up from the edge of the pool in which it was reflected.

But it was one of those human blossoms that Granville

knows so well how to paint, — with black locks, eyes
like stars, teeth like pearls, cheeks like peaches; the
whole enveloped, not by one of those thick, ill-advised
veils that conceal what they cover, but by a gauze so
fine, so silky, so transparent, that it seemed woven from
the filmy beams which Summer shakes from her distaff
when Autumn comes.

Then if the imprudent eye descended in a straight
line from her face, that was indeed another matter.
After a neck, which might have served as a model for
the Tower of Ivory of Scripture, came —

Undoubtedly what came after and was half hidden by
a chemise of white *maufe*, embroidered with blue, and
an *arkabouke* of cherry satin, was very beautiful, since
poor Iskander could not repress an exclamation of
delight.

The cry had no sooner escaped him than Iskander
wished that he had been born dumb; he had driven
himself out of Paradise.

The girl had heard the exclamation; she turned
around and uttered a cry on her part; over her transparent veil she threw a thick one, and ran, or, rather,
flew away, twice gasping the name of Iskander Beg.

He, stricken dumb when it was too late, motionless
when perhaps he would have run, his arms extended,
as if to stay the reality which, in fleeing, again melted
into a vision, stood breathless with staring eyes, like
Apollo watching the flight of Daphne.

But Apollo very quickly darted forth upon the track
of the beautiful nymph, while Iskander Beg did not
budge so long as he was able to catch a glimpse through
the thicket of a hand's breadth of that white veil.

And when it was lost to view he became much agitated, for he felt then as if life, a moment suspended,

**was** returning in waves upon him, rudely and noisily invading his heart.

"Allah!" murmured he, "what will they say of her and of me if any one has seen us? — How beautiful she is! — She will be scolded by her parents. — What lovely black eyes! — They will think that we had planned a rendezvous! — What lips! — She knows my name; twice as she ran she cried: 'Iskander! Iskander!'"

And he again sank into his revery, if a state can be called a revery in which the blood is boiling, while harps are ringing in one's ears, and when all the stars of heaven are seen in broad daylight.

Most certainly would night have surprised Iskander on the borders of the pool, into whose waters his heart seemed to have fallen, had not the horse, feeling his bridle, tightened for an instant, gently relax, continued on his way without consulting his rider.

Iskander reached home madly in love.

We are sorry indeed not to have found either time or space in this chapter to tell why Iskander bore malice to Mir Hadji Festahli; but we promise our readers, positively, to tell them in the following chapter.

## IV.

### IN WHICH ISKANDER LEARNS THE NAME OF HER WHO KNOWS HIS.

AND yet Iskander recalled his father's words. His father had been wont to say: " The loveliest rose lasts but a day, the smallest thorn endures a lifetime. Caress women, but do not love them if you would not become their slave. Love is sweet only in song; but in reality its beginning is fear; its middle, sin; and its end, repentance."

And to these three sentiments he added a fourth, their fitting complement: " Look not upon the wives of other men, and listen not to your own."

Let us hasten to add, to Iskander's credit, that he forgot all these precepts in less than five minutes.

The young Tartar loved and was afraid. The first part of his father's premonition, " The beginning of love is fear," was then fulfilled in him.

Eight days before, poor Iskander had slept so tranquilly, the night had seemed so short and refreshing.

Now he tossed about upon his mattress; he bit his pillow; his silk coverlet stifled him.

But who was *she?*

At this question, which he had put to himself for the tenth time, Iskander leaped from his bed to his feet.

*She!* what a villanous word!

Love tolerates no pronouns, and especially love in Daghestan.

Until he knew her true name, Iskander would give her a fictitious one.

"I must know the name of my — Leila," said he, thrusting his kandjiar into his girdle; "I shall die, perhaps, but I will know her name."

A moment later he was in the street.

Probably the devil left one of his serpents at Derbend: to some he takes the form of ambition, — how many celebrated men have disputed the possession of Derbend! to others he goes in the guise of love, — how many young people have lost their wits at Derbend!

The latter serpent, decidedly, had bitten Iskander Beg.

He wandered up and down the streets, looked through every gate, scanned every wall and every veil.

It was all in vain.

Whom could he ask for her name?   Who would point out her house?

His heart's eagerness urged him forward.

"Go!" it bade him.

Where?   He did not know.

He joined the crowd; the crowd conducted him to the market-place.

If he had wished to learn the price of meat, he was in a fair way: but the name of his beloved?   No!

He approached an Armenian.   The Armenians know everybody, dealing in everything.

This one was selling fish.

"Buy a fine *chamaia*, Iskander Beg," said the Armenian.

The young man turned away in disgust.

At last he approached the shop of a goldsmith, a skilful enameller.

"God save you!" said he to the Tartar.

3

"May Allah grant you happiness!" responded the goldsmith, without raising his eyes from a turquoise that he was mounting in a ring.

On the counter behind which the goldsmith was working stood a copper sebilla, filled with different objects more or less precious.

Iskander Beg uttered a cry.

He had just recognized an earring which he was certain of having seen, the day before, swinging in the ear of his unknown.

His heart gave a leap; it seemed to him that he had just learned the first letter of her name.

It was as if he saw her pretty little hand with the pink nails beckoning to him.

He dared not speak a word. He hesitated to put a question; he did not know what to say; his voice trembled, his thoughts were in a tumult.

Suddenly a light flashed across his brain.

He had hit upon a truly military ruse, — one of those that capture cities.

He emptied the cup into his hand, as if to look at the jewels. The goldsmith, who had recognized him, allowed him to do so.

He adroitly withdrew the earring from the heap of jewels, slipped it into his pocket, and suddenly ejaculated, —

"There! I have dropped an earring!"

And he replaced the other jewels in the cup.

"What earring?" demanded the merchant.

"The one with little bells on it."

"*Par Allah!* pick it up quickly, Iskander; I would not have that lost for five hundred roubles."

"Oh! it is not lost," said Iskander.

Then, after a pause, he said. —

"It is very strange, though, that I do not see it anywhere."

"One loses sight of a thing as it falls," said the merchant, laying down the ring upon which he was working; and rising, he looked under his bench as he raised his spectacles.

Iskander stepped about feigning to search.

"I do not find it," said he.

Then, a moment later, he added, —

"It is certainly lost."

This time the goldsmith took his spectacles from his forehead and laid them on his table.

"Allah!" he exclaimed, "what have you done, Iskander Beg?"

"I have lost an earring, that is all."

"But you don't know what will happen to me. That old rascal of a Hadji Festahli is capable of bringing suit against me. An earring of Baku enamel!"

"On my soul, you are laughing at me, Djaffar. Do you expect me to believe that a man as serious as Hadji Festahli, a descendant of Mahomet, a saint, wears earrings?"

"And who says that he wears earrings?"

"He has neither wife nor daughter, that I know of at least."

"He is too stingy for that, the old miser! But it is as much as ten years now since his brother Shafy fled into Persia, leaving him his wife and daughter. The little girl was only six years old then, she is sixteen now."

"It must be she! it must be she!" murmured Iskander under his breath.

Then he asked aloud, —

"What is she called — this niece?"

" Kassime," replied the goldsmith.

" Kassime, Kassime," repeated Iskander to himself.

And the name seemed to him far prettier than Leila, which he discarded as one throws away a lemon from which he has squeezed all the juice.

" And since her father's departure," he added aloud, " I presume that the little one has grown."

" You know our country, Iskander: the child of one year looks as though it were two; a girl of five appears to be ten. Our young girls are like the grape-cuttings which are scarcely planted before the grapes are ripe; I have never seen her, but her uncle says that she is the prettiest girl in Derbend."

Iskander Beg tossed the earring into the goldsmith's hand and darted off like an arrow. He knew all that he wished to know, — the name and dwelling of his lady fair.

He ran straight to the house of Hadji Festahli. He did not hope to see Kassime, but perhaps he should hear her voice; then, who knows? she might be going out with her mother, perhaps, and, whether he saw her or not, she would see him. She would certainly suspect that he was not there to get a glimpse of her uncle.

But, as usual, old Hadji Festahli's house was shut up; Iskander foresaw one drawback, — it was, in all Derbend, the most difficult house to enter.

He heard, not Kassime's voice, but a dog's bark, and it was redoubled every time that he drew near the gate. Finally, the gate opened.

But an abominable old hag emerged, broom in hand.

She was some old witch, doubtless, going to her vigil.

She did not even have the trouble of shutting the gate behind her; it closed quite of itself, one would have thought had he not heard a hand push the bolts.

Iskander had resolved to remain there until evening, until the next morning, until Kassime came out.   But his presence could not fail to be remarked, and his presence would announce openly to Hadji Festahli: "I love your niece; hide her more carefully than ever."

He returned home, and threw himself down upon a rug.

There, as he was no longer afraid of being seen or even heard, he threshed about, he roared, he bellowed.

Iskander loved after the manner of lions.

A good Mussulman, a true believer, has no conception of what we call perfect love; Iskander was purely enraged, he wanted Kassime that very moment, without delay, instantly.

He was one of the readers that skip the preface of a book and proceed immediately to the first chapter.

Terrible people for authors and uncles!

But Iskander very soon reached the conclusion that he might vainly roll on his rug all day long, roar a whole week, howl for a month, and it would not bring him a hair's breadth nearer to Kassime.

He must bestir himself, then.

Finally, by dint of saying over to himself: "Kassime's uncle," he was reminded that, if he himself had no uncle, he had an aunt.

An aunt!  Why were aunts made, if it were not to take charge of their nephew's love affairs?"

That is all aunts are good for.

You do not know of an aunt who ever served any other purpose; neither do I.

He went out and purchased some silk stuff for a dress; then he ran to his aunt's house.

The aunt took the dress, listened to the whole story of her nephew's love affair, and as an aunt, however old she may be, remembers the days when she was young, Iskander's aunt, sending a sigh after her own lost youth, promised him to do all in her power to bring about an interview.

"Come to my house to-morrow, at noon, my child," she said; "I will send for Kassime, under pretext of darkening her eyes with kohl. I will hide you behind this curtain, you rascal! But be discreet. Do not move, do not breathe, and, above all, beware of whispering a word to any one of what I am doing for you."

As one can well understand, Iskander returned home in high spirits.

He went to bed at sunset, hoping to sleep, and that the time would pass swiftly while he slept.

Sleep had been good once upon a time.

He fell asleep at one o'clock, and awoke at two.

By seven in the morning he was at his aunt's house, insisting that it was almost noon.

At every sound made at the gate he ran and hid behind the curtain.

Then he would resume his position beside his aunt, shaking his head and saying, —

"She will not come."

Whereupon, falling into a rage, and stamping his foot, he would exclaim, —

"Ah! if she does not come I will set fire to her uncle's house; she will have to come out so as not to be burned; then I will seize her, I will put her on my Karabach and run away with her."

And each time his aunt would soothe him, saying, —

"That could not have been she: it is only nine o'clock — it is only ten — it is only eleven."

But at noon the aunt exclaimed, —

"Ah! there she comes this time."

Iskander, like his aunt, had heard the heels of little Turkish slippers pattering on the paved court, and he had sprung behind his curtain.

It was indeed she, with her friend Kitchina, — blue-eyed Kitchina, as they called her.

The maidens took off their slippers at the threshold of the door and came in, seating themselves beside the old aunt.

The two veils fell to the floor.    The curtain was agitated; happily, neither of the girls looked that way.

No; they were watching the old aunt, who was stirring with a small ivory stick the kohl at the bottom of a little silver jar.

Kassime knelt before the good woman, who first pencilled her eyebrows, then the under-lids; but when Kassime, for the latter operation, raised her beautiful eyes, Iskander felt as if his heart were pierced by a bullet.

The old woman herself was struck with their wonderful beauty, and in her admiration for the girl, she said, embracing her, —

" How soon, my pretty Kassime, shall I be painting you in the bath amid the songs of your friends?    You have such beautiful eyes that I could wish them each morning to awake tearless and to be sealed every night by a kiss."

Kassime sighed, and affectionately kissed the old woman.

Iskander heard the sigh and felt the warmth of the kiss.

" My uncle Festahli says that I am too young," answered Kassime, sadly.

" And what says your heart? " demanded the old lady.

Instead of replying, Kassime took down the tam·
bourine hanging on the wall, and sang: —

> " Fair dawn, oh, why did I so early feel
>     The dewy coolness of thy wings ?
> Fair youth, oh, why this eve did thine eyes steal
>     Into my heart their fiery stings ?

> " Oh, why, though I have seen in cloudless sky
>     Enthroned the god-like shining star, —
> Oh, why, though I have seen from storm-cloud high
>     A serpent fire o'erleap heaven's bar, —

> " Oh, why, since I 've forgotten dreaded woes
>     And longed-for weal, sad earth, gay skies —
> So much forgotten, sun and fire, dawn's rose —
>     Oh, why forget I not thine eyes ? "

While singing the last verse of the song which she
was improvising, Kassime blushed to her shoulders;
then, laughing like a child, she dropped her tambourine
and threw herself into her friend's arms; and then the
two silly young things both began to laugh.

Why were they laughing, and what was there so
laughable in all that?

But Iskander's aunt understood very well, and, for
the sake of her nephew's happiness, she determined to
bring out the secret of the enigma immediately.

" O my sweet rose," she said, playing with Kassime's
rings, " if my nephew could have heard the song you
have just sung, he would have staved in the wall to see
the singer, and after seeing her, he would have carried
her off as a lion does a kid."

And just then a jar filled with jasmin water fell from
the chest that stood near the curtain and broke into a
thousand pieces.

The old woman faced about; the two young people turned pale.

" Why did it fall ? " asked Kassime in trembling tones.

" That devil of a black cat! " exclaimed the old lady; " there was never another like it! "

Kassime was reassured.

" Oh, I detest black cats! " said she.  " It is said that they sometimes lend their skin to the devil, and that is why we can see their eyes glare in the dark."

Then turning to her friend, she said, —

" Come, Kitchina, mamma allowed me but an hour, and there is the mullah's call."

Kassime rather coldly embraced the old woman, who saw that the reserve was assumed.

" Nonsense! " said the aunt, accompanying her to the door, " it is useless for you to be angry, Kassime.  I should like to see you with flowers upon your head; your happiness is as dear to me as a link of gold, and with a link of gold, I know a young man who would like to bind his soul to yours.   But be at ease, my dear child, only Allah, he, and I know the secret."

Kassime opened her great eyes, whose size was doubled with amazement, but she was just then at the threshold of the street-door; her friend, who was behind, pushed her gently, the door was shut, and, for all explanation, she heard the key creaking in the lock.

Iskander Beg fairly stifled his aunt in his arms when she returned from Kassime.  The good woman scolded him well because he had not been able to keep still at his post of observation.

" Oh! " she exclaimed, " when that dreadful jar fell I nearly died from fright!   Wicked child! it would have been the death of me if Kassime had guessed who made it fall."

"Is it my fault, aunt?" cried Iskander; "and could I keep quiet when my heart threatened to burst at sight of the roses that overspread Kassime's cheeks after you had spoken of me? I longed to gather them with my lips. What could you expect? Who sows must reap!"

"Not when he sows in another's garden."

"Then buy me this garden, aunt; do not let me expire like a nightingale on the thorns of a rose-bush. Kassime must be my wife; ask her uncle for her, then, without delay, and rest assured that I shall be as grateful as I am loving. Succeed in your embassy, dear aunt, and I promise you the most beautiful pair of buffaloes in Daghestan."

On the morrow Iskander Beg received the answer of Mir Hadji Festahli.

Alas! it was very far from being what he had hoped.

Here it is, for that matter; the reader can judge how much of hope it left to poor Iskander.

"Tell your Iskander, for me," Festahli had replied to the aunt, "that I have not forgotten his father. His father was a brute. One day, before everybody, he called me, — I will not repeat what he called me; I could take no revenge, because it was just at the time when the Russians were interfering with our customs; but I have not forgotten the offence. I have not burned his coffin. It is proper for the son to pay his father's debt, and I am no dog to fawn on the hand that has beaten me. But, to tell the truth, had there been no feud between us, Iskander should not have had my niece in any case. A great honor to be the uncle of this beg! There are seventy begs in Derbend just like him; I will give him their names whenever he likes. Why talk to me of a dowry? Yes, faith, by ruining himself, he could pay for my niece; but after that

how would he provide for her? Has he any relatives
to help him in case of need? How many raven's-eggs
does he get from the rent of his huts? How many
bundles of nettles has he reaped in his fields? He is
destitute, utterly destitute, your beggar of a nephew.
Tell him no, — a hundred times no. I will not have
such a good-for-nothing as he is in my family. A head
and a purse so empty that with only a breath both
head and purse would fly away. Good-evening, old
woman!"

With the knowledge that you already possess of
Iskander Beg's disposition, you can imagine his rage
when his aunt brought him this answer, word for word.

At last, his wrath cooled; and he had sworn to be
terribly revenged upon Mir Hadji Festahli.

He was a Tartar.

This explains why Hadji Festahli was so preoccupied
while climbing the streets which led to the dwelling of
Iskander Beg; why, in his preoccupation, he spat upon
the black beard of Hussein and the red beard of Ferzali,
and why, at last, arrived at Iskander Beg's door, instead
of knocking impatiently, he knocked very gently.

## V.

### A BARGAIN.

ISKANDER was neither rich nor married : his door, therefore, was quickly opened, not half way, but wide open ;
for he had no fear that in coming to see him people
would see either his wife or his strong-box.

Hence Iskander received his visitors, not on the
threshold, as do Mussulmans who are fathers of a family,
but in his innermost room. There was nothing in his
house to tempt the pilferer of either hearts or money.

" Welcome ! " he cried from the other side of the door
to the arrivals, even before knowing who they were.

And the door was opened.

Iskander Beg himself had come to let them in, as his
noukar was grooming his horse. He stood amazed at be-
holding Mir Hadji Festahli and his associates in the
street.

The blood rushed to his head, and his first impulse was
to feel for his dagger.

But, thanks to a violent effort, curiosity overcame the
anger within him.

He respectfully placed his hand upon his heart, bowed
to his visitors, and invited them to enter.

They seated themselves upon the rugs, stroked their
beards with oriental gravity, regulated the folds of their
garments, and the conversation opened with common-
places.

Finally, after five minutes lost in trivialities, Mir Hadji Festahli broached the question.

He spoke of the misfortunes which threatened Daghestan in general and the town of Derbend in particular, if such a drouth should continue eight days longer.

At every pause he turned to his companions, as if to ask their support ; but it was now their turn to be silent, and if they spat not upon his beard, it was certainly not the desire that was lacking.

Iskander, on his part, appeared very little moved at the pathetic picture that Mir Hadji Festahli drew of the hardships of the city and province ; but from the flush on his face it could be seen that a fire was smouldering in his bosom.

Finally, Hadji Festahli rounded up his discourse with this threefold lamentation · —

" Woe ! woe ! woe to Derbend ! "

" Probably ! " answered Iskander.

" Certainly ! " added Hussein.

" Absolutely ! " whimpered Ferzali.

After which ensued a moment of silence.

During this pause Iskander looked from one to another of his visitors with questioning glance ; but they were dumb.

Iskander began to be impatient.

" You have not come, brethren," said he, " that we might wipe away our perspiration and shed our tears together, and I presume that, on your part, or on the part of those that sent you, — for you impress me as being ambassadors to my august presence, — you have something to say to me of more importance than what you have communicated."

" Our brother is possessed of great penetration," returned Hadji Festahli, inclining his head.

And then, with an abundance of oriental circumlocu-
tion on the honor to Iskander of being the object of such
a choice, he recounted what the inhabitants of Derbend
were expecting from his devotedness.

But at that, Iskander's brow began to cloud threat-
eningly.

" Strange choice ! " he cried with emphasis.  " Until
now the inhabitants of Derbend, for whom, however, I
have fought tolerably well, — though it is true that I
fought on my own behalf rather than theirs, — not only
have not spoken to me, but they have hardly saluted me.
And here they offer me a commission which I was not
soliciting and of which I am unworthy.  It is true that
there are many precipices on the heights of Schach
Dagh ; true, too, that in the gorges of Schach Dagh are
the haunts of the brigand Mullah Nour, that there are ten
chances to one of my rolling over a precipice, and twenty
to one of my being killed by Mullah Nour; but little it
matters to them, — I can be of use to them in this, and
they have turned to me.  And why, pray, should I, who
love warmth and sunshine, ask Allah for clouds and
rain ?  On the contrary, I am delighted that my house is
dry, my stable wholesome, and that there is neither fog
in the air nor mud in the street.  Besides, the sun
hatches my raven's-eggs, and my nettles grow well without rain.  You scoffed because I have no grain to reap !
Why, having no grain, should I disturb myself about
yours ?  You have maligned my father, you have robbed
him, you have persecuted him, you have scorned me, and
now, you wish me to risk my life for your sake, and to
pray God to have mercy upon you !  But I mistake, —
doubtless it is for some new affront that you come to me,
and, that nothing may be wanting to the insult, the task
of making me such a proposition has been confided to

this holy man, the respectable Hadji Festahli. They do not load the camel when he is on his feet, but when he kneels ; and I, pray observe, am on my feet."

And Iskander stood as haughty as a king, as terrible as a god.

"Now," said he, " we have a little matter to settle, Hadji Festahli and I. We will absent ourselves a few moments ; excuse us, worthy lords ! "

And he beckoned Hadji Festahli to follow him into an adjoining room.

Thereupon the face of the holy Mussulman became as long and sombre as a night in autumn. He arose smiling ; but, as every one knows, there are two kinds of smiles ; one puts out the lips as if to kiss, the other shows the teeth as if to bite.

They passed together into the next room.

What black-bearded Hussein and red-bearded Ferzali were talking about meanwhile, we are unable to tell our readers, because we were listening at the keyhole of the room to which Hadji Festahli and Iskander had retired.

The two enemies returned in a short time with radiant faces ; they looked like the two diamond-set medals of the Lion and the Sun, hung side by side on the breast of a Persian Minister.

Iskander then turned to his other guests and said : —

"At first I had certain motives, best known to myself, for not conforming to the desires of the people of Derbend ; but the honorable Hadji Festahli, whom God preserve, has given me such excellent reasons for complying that I am now ready to go and bring the snow from the summit of Schach Dagh, at the risk of plunging over precipices and getting my moustache singed by Mullah Nour. Allah is all-powerful, and if an earnest, fervent prayer can touch his heart, I venture to prophesy that it

will soften, and that the very clouds will weep so many
tears that the earth's thirst will be quenched not only for
this year, but for a year to come.    I set out this evening.
Pray, — I will act."

Then he added : —

" Time is precious, I will not detain you."

The ambassadors thanked Iskander ; their feet glided
into their slippers and the visitors were gone.

Iskander was left alone ; it was what he wanted.

" Well," cried he, joyfully, when he was sure that no
one could hear him, " he is a little better than I took him
to be, that old knave of a Hadji Festahli.    He could
have killed me because my father, one day, before everybody, had called him a son of — no matter what ! and
now, like a true patriarch, he sacrifices his resentment for
the public good, and gives me his niece in exchange for a
little snow.    Excellent man, that ! "

Hussein   and   Ferzali,   as   they   went   away,   were
saying : —

" That Iskander is not a man, but an angel.    He was
furious against Derbend, enraged against Festahli ; but
when we had spoken of the wailing and suffering of the
poor, he could refuse us no longer."

And as for the people, overjoyed that Iskander had
given his consent, they began to dance and sing.

Festahli — laughed in his sleeve.

" A promise, a promise ! " murmured he.    " What is a
promise, especially when no witnesses are by ?   He cannot hold me to it ; I should have died of shame if I had
gone before the people with Iskander's refusal.    And besides, I added, ' If your journey ends happily.'    Now,
Iskander has not returned, the paths of Schach Dagh are
very steep, and Mullah Nour is very brave.    We shall
see !   We shall see ! "

A very holy man was Mir Hadji Festahli Ismaël *Ogli* !
He was a direct descendant of the prophet.

Iskander kissed his good Karabach from very joy,
saying : —

"They are fools, on my word of honor, to suppose that
I am doing all this for the sake of their wheat. Ah ! for
Kassime, for my beloved, for my adored Kassime, I
would climb not only Schach Dagh, but the moon be
sides ! Ibrahim ! Give my horse some oats. Oats ! "

## VI.

### A DISSERTATION ON THE NOSE.

HAVE you ever considered, dear reader, what an admi rable organ is the nose?

The nose, yes, the nose!

And how useful is the nose to every creature that lifts, as Ovid says, his face to heaven?

Ah, well, strange to say, — ingratitude unparalleled! — not a poet has yet thought of addressing an ode to the nose!

It has remained for me, who am not a poet, or who, at least, claim only to rank after our great poets, to conceive such an idea.

Truly, the nose is unfortunate.

Men have invented so many things for the eyes!

They have made them songs, compliments, kaleido scopes, pictures, scenery, spectacles.

And for the ears:

Earrings, first of all, *Robert the Devil*, *William Tell*, *Fra Diavolo*, Stradivarius violins, Érard pianos, Sax trumpets.

And for the mouth:

*Carême*, *The Plain Cook*, *The Gastronomist's Calendar*, *The Gourmand's Dictionary*. They have made it soups of every kind, from the Russian *batwigne* to the French cabbage-soup; they have garnished its dishes with the reputations of the greatest men, from cutlets *à la Soubise* to puddings *à la Richelieu;* they have compared its lips to coral, its teeth to pearls, its breath to benzoin ; they have set before it peacocks in their plumes, snipes undrawn; finally, for the future they promise it larks roasted whole.

What has been invented for the nose ?

Attar of roses, and snuff.

Ah! that is not well, O philanthropists, my masters! O poets, my confrères !

And yet with what fidelity this member —

"It is not a member !" cry the savants.

Pardon, messieurs, I take it back : this appendage — Ah ! And yet, as I was saying, with what fidelity has this appendage served you !

The eyes go to sleep, the mouth closes, the ears are deaf.

The nose, alone, is always on duty.

It guards your repose, contributes to your health. All other parts of your body, the feet, the hands, are stupid. The hands let themselves be caught in the act, like the fools they are ; the feet stumble and let the body fall, like the clumsy creatures that they are.

And, in the latter case, who suffers for it, generally ? The feet commit the fault, and the nose takes the punishment.

How often do you hear it said, —

Monsieur So-and-so has broken his nose !

There have been a great many broken noses since the creation of the world.

Can any one cite a single nose whose fault it was ?

No. Everything assaults the poor nose.

Well, it endures all with angelic patience. True, it sometimes has the hardihood to snore. But where and when did you ever hear it complain ?

We forget that nature created it an admirable instru
ment for increasing or decreasing the volume of the
voice. We say nothing of the service it renders us in
acting as a medium between our souls and the souls of
flowers. Let us repress its utility and regard it only from
its æsthetic side, that of beauty.

A cedar of Lebanon, it tramples underfoot the hyssop
of the moustache ; a central column, it provides a support
for the double arch of the eyebrows. On its capital
perches the eagle of thought. It is enwreathed with
smiles. With what intrepidity did the nose of Ajax con-
front the storm when he said, " 1 will escape in spite of
the gods ! " With what courage did the nose of the
great Condé — who would never have been great except
for his nose — with what courage did the nose of the
great Condé enter before all others, before the great
Condé himself, the entrenchments of the Spaniards at
Lens and Rocroy, where their conqueror had been so
bold, or, rather, so rash as to flourish his bâton of command ? With what assurance was thrust before the public Dugazon's nose, which knew forty-two ways of
wriggling, and each funnier than the last !

No, I do not believe that the nose should be con-
demned to the obscurity into which man's ingratitude has
hitherto forced it.

Perhaps, also, it is because the noses of the Occident
are so small, that they have submitted to this injustice.

But the deuce is to pay if there are none but Occi-
dental noses !

There are the Oriental noses, which are very handsome
noses.

Do you question the superiority of these noses over
your own, gentlemen of Paris, of Vienna, of Saint
Petersburg ?

In that case, Viennese, take the Danube ; Parisians, the steamer ; Peterbourgeois, the *perecladdoï*, and say these simple words : —

"To Georgia ! "

Ah ! but I forewarn you of a deep humiliation ; should you bring to Georgia one of the largest noses in Europe, — Hyacinthe's nose or Schiller's, — at the gate of Tiflis they would gaze at you with astonishment and exclaim :

" This gentleman has lost his nose on the way, — what a pity ! "

At the first street in the town, — what am I saying ! at the first house in the faubourg, you would be convinced that all other noses, Greek, Roman, German, French, Spanish, Neopolitan even, should bury themselves in the bowels of the earth with chagrin at sight of the Georgian noses.

Ah ! blessed God ! Those beautiful Georgian noses ! robust noses ! magnificent noses !

To begin with, there are all shapes.

Round, fat, long, large.

There is every kind.

White, pink, red, violet.

Some are set with rubies, others with pearls ; I saw one that was set with turquoises.

You have only to squeeze them between two fingers, and a pint, at the very least, of Kakhetia wine will flow.

In Georgia, Vakhtang IV. abolished the fathom, the metre, the archine ; he retained but the nose.

Goods are measured off by the nose.

They say :  "I bought seventeen noses of termalama for a dressing-gown, seven noses of kanaos for a pair of trousers, a nose and a half of satin for a cravat."

And, let us add, the Georgian dames find this measure more convenient than the European measures.

But, in the matter of noses, Daghestan is not to be sneezed at.

Thus, for instance, in the centre of the face of a Derbend beg, Hadji Yussef, — God give strength to his shoulders ! arose a certain protuberance for which his compatriots are still hunting a suitable name, although some call it a trumpet, some a rudder, others a handle !

In its shade three men could sleep.

One can understand how such a nose would be greatly respected at Derbend during a hot spell of fifty-two degrees in the sun, since on the other side of this nose, that is to say in the shade, it was but forty degrees.

We need not be greatly surprised, then, that Yussef had been assigned to Iskander as a guide.

But let us confess the whole truth : it was not entirely on account of his nose that he had been appointed.

As indicated by the title Hadji, prefixed to Yussef's name, Yussef had made the pilgrimage to Mecca.

In order to get there, he had traversed Persia, Asia Minor, Palestine, the Desert, a part of Arabia Petræa, and a portion of the Red Sea.

And, on his return, wonderful tales did Yussef tell of his travels, of dangers encountered, of bandits slain, of wild beasts whose jaws he had broken like a Samson !

Whenever he appeared at the bazaar of Derbend, people stepped aside, saying, —

" Make way for the lion of the steppe ! "

" He is a remarkable man ! " assented the most pointed moustaches and the longest beards, as Yussef Beg turned their heads with the current of his plausible speech. It was said that in going over the summit of a mountain in Persia, his papak had caught on the horn of the moon, the mountain was so high ; that for a long time, his sole nourishment had been derived from omelettes of eagles'

eggs ; and that he had passed nights in caverns where,
when he sneezed, the echo itself had responded, " God
bless you ! "

It is true that he spoke without reflection for the
greater part of the time ; but when he did speak, his
words supplied food for reflection to others.   What beasts
had he not seen !   What men had he not met !   He had
seen animals having two heads and a single foot, he had
met men who had no heads and who thought with their
stomachs.

All these tales were really a little old ; doubtless that
was why no one had thought of sending him for the ball
of snow ; but when by common consent this commission
had fallen to Iskander, Yussef mounted his Persian steed,
put his Andrev poniard, his Kouba pistol and Vladikafkaz
schaska in his girdle, and rode proudly through the
streets of Derbend, proclaiming, —

" If you like, I will accompany poor Iskander ; for how
do you imagine poor Iskander can get along without me ? "

The people answered, —

" Ah, very well ; accompany Iskander."

Then he went home to reinforce his defensive armor
with a breastplate of copper links, his offensive armor
with a Nouka gun.   Yellow boots with high heels com-
pleted his costume ; last of all, he suspended whip and
sabre from his saddle.

He could hardly stir in the midst of his arsenal.

He was ready long before Iskander, and awaited him at
the city gates, declaiming : —

" Well ! will he never come ?   If they had selected
me I should have been off two hours ago."

About six o'clock in the afternoon, Iskander issued
from his court on his Karabach horse, wearing the cos
tume and arms with which all were familiar.

Iskander traversed the city slowly, — not that he had the least intention in the world of exhibiting himself, but because the streets leading from his house to the gates of Derbend were thronged with people.

At last, he succeeded in joining Yussef Beg, gave him his hand, saluted for a last time the inhabitants of Derbend and set off at a gallop.

Yussef followed on a Khorassan charger. For some time horses and riders could be distinguished, then only the dust, then nothing at all.

Horses and riders had disappeared.

Arrived at a vast cemetery, Iskander Beg slackened his Karabach's pace.

Night began to fall.

But Iskander heeded neither night nor cemetery; he was dreaming of his darling Kassime.

Yussef kept glancing to right and left with a certain degree of uneasiness, and he profited by Iskander's slackening speed to approach him.

Iskander was plunged in thought.

Ah ! if you have ever been youthful in soul, if you have ever loved with all your heart, and if, youthful and loving, you have been going far away from the place where lives your dear one, you will then understand what feelings were uppermost in the breast of Iskander Beg. It is folly, doubtless, to imagine that in breathing the same atmosphere we have the same dreams ; that in gazing ten times at a window, although it be shut, we bring away ten memories ; but this folly is solacing. Fancy is always more picturesque than fact : fancy is poetry ; it flies, light as bird or angel, and never are its white wings sullied with either mud or dust from the highway.

Fact, on the contrary, is prose : it plunges into details ;

while clinging round the bride's fair neck it fails to note the delicacy of her skin, but asks itself if the pearls of her necklace are real or false, if she makes love to her husband, pets her dog, or gives money to the servants.

*Ma foi!* long live poetry!

Iskander was making very nearly the same reflections as ourselves, — but he at least was making them at twenty-five, which necessarily imparted to them both the colors of the rose and the perfume of May-bloom, — when he felt himself touched on the elbow by Yussef Beg.

"Well," he asked, emerging from his revery, "what is it, Yussef?"

"Merely that, as we have not seen fit to stay in the city with the living, I see no reason why we should remain in a cemetery with the dead. How I would burn their graves, did not every stone appear to be rising, and were not that she-devil of a gallows stretching out her lean black hand toward us!"

"She is longing for you, Hadji Yussef; she fears that you may escape her," laughed Iskander.

"I spit on the beard of him that put her there," said Hadji Yussef. "Allah protect me! but whenever I pass this place, good Mussulman as I believe myself to be, pure of heart as I think I am, it always seems to me as if she were about to clutch me by the throat; and avow the truth, Iskander, confess that if we were not under Russian rule we should not remain very long in the city, foot in the stirrup and gun on the shoulder. Down with the troops! Ah! but I should like to settle those troops, — I would hack them into bits no larger than millet-seed!"

"Really, my dear Yussef, I did not know you were so brave at night. At the time of Kasi Mullah's attack, I saw how you fought in the day-time, or rather I did not see you: were you not in Derbend?"

" Ah, now ! my dear Iskander, you are always making
fun of me !   Did I not indeed in your own presence cut
off the head of that Lesghian, who was so enraged against
me that his head, after it had fallen to the earth, bit my
foot so cruelly that I suffer from it to this very day every
time the weather changes ?   What ! seriously, did you
not see that ? "

" Allah denied me that pleasure."

" Besides, are those Lesghians men ?   Is it worth
while to pit one's head against their balls ?   If I kill a
Lesghian, it matters little ; but, if a Lesghian kills me,
Allah will find it difficult to fill my place.   So, after I
had killed that one, I thought it quite enough of hand-
to-hand combat.   I went into the citadel every day : I
appropriated a cannon ; yes, I constituted myself its
artillery-man, I aimed it and I gave the gunner the order,
' Fire ! ' and then I saw some dancing in the group at
which I had pointed my gun.   Ah ! Allah !   I had great
sport.   I have never boasted of it, but I can say this to
you as a friend ; I am sure that I was the principal cause,
in view of the damage that I did, of Kasi Mullah's raising
the siege ; and when you reflect that I have never received
a single cross, not even that of Saint George —   Eh ! do
you not hear something ? " added the valiant Beg, shrink-
ing against Iskander.

" What the devil could you hear in this place, except
the whistling wind and howling jackals ? "

" Cursed brutes !   I could kill their fathers, mothers,
and grandparents.   What wake are they keeping now,
I want to know."

" Perhaps they expect to feast to-morrow night on our
carcasses.   You know, really, Yussef, that the one that
captures your nose will be in luck."

" Come, come, no sinful jesting, Iskander !   Ill word

brings ill work. This is the very hour for brigands. When night comes, the devils walk the highways. Iskander, what if we should meet Mullah Nour?"

"Who is Mullah Nour?" said Iskander, as if he had never heard the name that his fellow-traveller had just pronounced.

"Not so loud, Iskander! not so loud, I beg of you in the names of Hussein and Ali, or I swear I will not stay with you. This cursed Mullah Nour has ears in every tree; just when you are not thinking of him — crash! he falls on your head like a thunderbolt."

"And then?"

"How 'and then'?"

"I ask, what happens afterwards?"

"Afterwards you are caught. He likes to laugh and joke, but, you understand, with a brigand's pleasantry. If he knows you to be miserly he will first take all that you have in your pockets, without counting the ransom that he will put on your head. From another, if he is poor, he will take nothing; he will even give."

"What! he will give?"

"Yes, there have been such instances. Fine fellows who are in love and who have not twenty-five roubles to buy them a wife, — well, he gives them the money. From some he will take in gold the weight of the shot in his cartridges; of others still, he will demand as many roubles as he can hold on the blade of his sword. 'What would you have?' says he; 'I am myself a poor merchant, and every trade has its risks, especially mine.'"

"But," laughed Iskander, "those whom he stops must carry pipes instead of guns. Or is Mullah Nour made of iron?"

"Of iron? Say rather of steel, my friend. Balls flatten against him as against granite. Allah is great!"

"After what you tell me, Yussef, I am inclined to think that Mullah Nour is the devil in person. He must be the devil instead of a man, to be able to stop whole caravans."

"Ah! one can see, poor boy, that you have never heard anything but the crowing of your own cock! And who, pray, says that Mullah Nour has no comrades? Why, on the contrary, he is surrounded by a parcel of knaves who think it better to eat bread raised by others than to be at the pains of raising their own. Comrades! By Allah! he is not wanting for comrades. Why, I myself, for instance, have often thought of it. If I had no relatives, no inheritance to expect, brave and adventurous— But what is the matter now, Iskander? Where are you going at that gait? They say that night is the devil's day, and I am beginning to believe it, for this night is as black as hell. But answer me, Iskander; what are you thinking about?"

"I am thinking that you are a bad soldier, Hadji Yussef."

"I, a bad soldier? Aren't you ashamed to say such a thing to me? It is to be regretted that you were not present when I settled a band of brigands near Damascus. I can say without boasting that after I had saved them the whole caravan of pilgrims was at my feet, and with good reason, too. I killed so many that my gun waxed red-hot and went off of itself. As for my sword, it was in pretty shape; it had teeth like a comb. I left seven dead on the field of battle and took two alive."

"What did you do with them?"

"I burned them the next morning; they were in the way."

"That was savage, Yussef."

"What can you expect? I am as I am."

"And you can tell me such tales without blushing?
Your musket had more conscience than you; it turned
red, at any rate."

"You do not believe me? Ask Sapharkouli; he was
there."

"How unfortunate that Sapharkouli died eight days
ago!"

"True. As if he could not have waited, the fool!
Well, well! but, according to you, I must be a pol-
troon. *Par Allah!* Set me face to face with a dozen
brigands, and you shall see how I will settle them.
Come, where are they? Point your finger at them, —
but not at night. Oh! I don't like to fight at night.
I want the sun to shine on my valor; and then, I have
a habit of taking aim with my right eye."

"I cannot recover from my surprise, Yussef. A dozen
brigands, and you will consider them your affair?"

"I will make a breakfast of them."

"Let day come, then, and may we meet a dozen
brigands, — a round dozen. I promise to leave them to
you, Yussef. I will not touch one, not even with the
hilt of my dagger."

"My dear, never wish to see the devil, lest he immediately appear. Now, as brigands are devils, and as we
are here on their ground, it is best not to invoke them.
For that matter, it gets darker and darker. Satan must
have made off with the moon. Cursed night! how it
drags! Ah! help! help!"

"What ails you?"

"A brigand has caught me, Iskander! Let me go,
demon!"

"Stand aside, and I will fire."

"Stand aside, stand aside! that is very easily said.
I believe he has claws. He has got me as a hawk holds

its prey.  Who are you?  What do you want?  Come,
friend, let us make terms."

Iskander approached Yussef.

"I suspected as much," said he.  "Fear has big eyes;
your brigand is a thorn bush.  Oh, my dear Yussef,
you ought to have ridden an ass to the fountain for
water, instead of coming with me to get snow on the
top of Schach Dagh."

"A bush?  I swear that it was certainly a Lesghian
or Tchetchen; but he saw me put my hand on my
poniard, and he loosed his grip."

"He saw you put your hand on your poniard in such
darkness as this, when you yourself say the devil has
run away with the moon?"

"Those knaves are like cats; it is well known that
they can see in the dark.  Oh! my dear Iskander, what
is that in front of us?"

"It is the river.  What! with a nose like yours, can
you not scent water?  See, my horse knows more than
you."

"Do you mean to cross the river to-night?"

"Certainly."

"Iskander, you are undertaking a very imprudent
thing.  Better wait till to-morrow, Iskander.  It is
no trifling matter to cross the river at this hour, and
the Karatcha, too!"

Iskander was already in the middle of the stream.

Yet Yussef preferred to follow his companion rather
than to stay behind; he plunged into the black river,[1]
and, after exclaiming at the coldness of the water, after
shrieking that he was being dragged down by the feet,
after calling Allah to witness that he was a lost man,
Yussef finally reached the opposite bank.

[1] Karatcha means black river.

The comrades resumed their journey and crossed successively the Alcha and the Velvet.

At daybreak they had reached the banks of the Samour.

The Samour flowed swiftly; they saw enormous boulders roll with the waves, and uprooted trees were following its current, floating on the surface like so many wisps of straw on a brooklet.

This time Iskander yielded to Yussef's advice, and halted.

The riders dismounted to give their horses time to rest, they themselves lying down upon their bourkas.

But Yussef was not the man to go to sleep without relating some of his daring deeds.

Iskander listened this time, neither interrupting him nor laughing at him. He was falling asleep.

The one told of what had never taken place.

The other dreamed of what was to come.

At last, finding himself without support in the conversation, Yussef decided to go to sleep.

Iskander had been asleep a long time.

## VII.

### MULLAH NOUR.

It is delightful to be awakened by the sun's first ray,
as it peeps through a silk curtain, and lifts the black
covering of night from the face of the wife sleeping
near you, as fresh as the dewdrop on the leaf.   But it
is more delightful still, after a short sleep, to open the
eyes under a cloudless sky and find yourself face to face
with the smiling countenance of Nature.   The *fiancée*
is always more beautiful than the wife; and what is
Nature, if not the eternal *fiancée* of man?

Iskander slowly raised his eyelids, still weighted
with dreams, and admired the splendid picture of the
morning.    All around him undulated the forest, rich
with its Southern verdure; above his head glittered and
smoked the snowy peak of Schach Dagh.   At his feet
rolled the noisy Samour, sometimes leaping in cascades,
sometimes winding its waves into great coils, like a
serpent writhing amidst the rocks.

On the banks of the channel where the river roared,
the nightingale sang.

Iskander enjoyed a brief moment of enchantment;
but just as the bird was renewing an interrupted song,
a terrible snore from Yussef roused him to reality.

The sleeper's nose projected from his bourka, whose
surface it overshot by two or three inches.

Iskander shook Yussef by the nose and awoke him.

"Hallo! Who goes there?" demanded Yussef, speedily opening his eyes. "Ah! it is you. May the devil fly away with you!" was his greeting to Iskander on recognizing him. "Is a man to be rung by the nose as a Russian official rings a bell to summon his aids? Know, Iskander, that when Allah favors a man by giving him such a nose, it is that he may command respect and admiration from others. I admire and respect my nose; share my sentiments in this regard, or we shall have a falling out."

"My dear Yussef, excuse me; but when I am in haste I seize a man by the first part of him that comes to hand. The first — I will even say the only part of you that I saw, the rest being hidden under your bourka — happened to be your nose, and I took hold of it."

"Iskander, my friend, some day we shall quarrel, and that day, I foresee, will be a sorry one for you. What the deuce was the matter? Out with it!"

"I was vexed at that confounded nightingale, whose singing interfered with my listening to your snore. Why, my dear Yussef, you snore so musically that, compared with the melodies that you play naturally in your sleep, the Georgian djourna's performance is like a penny trumpet's."

"Ah, yes, appease me now. But may you all your life feed only on the odor of roses, and have all their thorns in the soles of your boots, if ever — "

Iskander interrupted him.

"Do you not hear something, Yussef?" he asked.

Yussef listened uneasily.

"No, nothing," said he, after a pause; "nothing but the voice of the mullah at Seyfouri."

"Well, what says the voice, Yussef? 'Wake ye, faithful Mussulmans; prayer is better than sleep.' We

5

have a journey to make, Yussef; let us pray and be
setting forth."

Yussef yielded to the invitation, although with grum-
bling.    It seemed to him that Iskander had yielded
ground in the discussion, — an event happening with
them so rarely that he would gladly have profited by
his comrade's frame of mind.

Having performed their ablutions and their prayers,
our travellers made ready to ford the river.

The water was not unusually high; yet it is admitted
by those who are acquainted with mountain torrents,
and especially with the Samour, that the fording of a
river is always more perilous than a battle.

Everything depends, in such a case, upon your horse;
if he makes a misstep, you are lost.    But habit renders
travellers indifferent to these dangers, although, every
year, more than one is left at the ford forever.

Our two begs, thanks to their skill, to their acquaint-
ance with this sort of exercise, and especially to the
excellence of their horses, reached the opposite bank of
the Samour safe and sound.

Yussef, who had been as mute as a tench during the
whole time of their crossing, began to scold again the
very instant that he touched the farther bank.

"May the devil take this river!" said he; "I will
heave a pig at it!   And to think that it is so dry during
the autumn and winter that a frog crossing it could not
manage to wash his feet!"

"Where shall we stop in Seyfouri?" inquired
Iskander, without heeding the tirades of his comrade,
who, the danger past, had already forgotten it.   "I do
not know a living soul there; yet there our horses must
breakfast, and so must we."

"I will burn their beards with a wisp of straw, — the

blackguards!" responded Yussef. "It is very clear that, without an order from the governor, not one of them will offer us a drop of water, or even a radish, if they see us drop down with hunger and thirst."

"The people of Seyfouri are neither better nor worse than those of Derbend; but when it comes to that, we are all Tartars."

"Here we are! we shall see. Perhaps with a little money we can get something from them. As we ride along, look well on your side into the courts; I will keep watch on mine. Perhaps we shall come across a grey-beard; the grey-beards are better than the red ones. The grey-beard is a starost, while the red-beard is a rich man. The red-beard almost always has money and a pretty wife, — two reasons for shutting his doors in the faces of two handsome fellows like us. And here is just the man I was looking for. Hey! friend," continued Yussef, addressing a grey-beard, "can we rest an hour at your house, and have a bite to eat?"

"Are you on government service?" demanded the man, a tall, dark-hued Tartar.

"No, my friend, no."

"Have you an order from the governor?"

"We have money, nothing more."

"That is sufficient to obtain a welcome in my house; I receive many lords from Khorassan, and, thanks be to Allah, never have horse or horseman had reason to complain of Agraïne."

The gates were thrown open; the travellers entered the court, dismounted, unsaddled their horses, and gave them oats.

Let us say, in passing, that the people of Daghestan are remarkably neat, and usually have two-story houses of brick white-washed with lime

Agraïne's house was one of these. He invited his guests to ascend to the first floor.

Yussef required no urging, and led the way for Iskander.

At the door of the first room, Agraïne took their arms and set them against the wall, as a sign that, being in his house it was now his duty to provide for their safety.

This custom is so widespread that our two travellers opposed no resistance.

Within this room they saw nothing but a pair of woman's trousers.

Nothing so irritates an Asiatic, and, in general, a Mussulman, whoever he may be, as a question about his wife.

Hadji Yussef was dying to question his host about those trousers; but Agraïne was the owner of one of those faces that check raillery on the lips of the jester.

" Have you not a pinch of pilaff to offer us, my friend ? " he asked the Tartar.

" The prophet himself never ate the like of that my wife used to prepare," answered Agraïne.  " Allah! my guests wore out their fingers with licking them, it was so rich."

" What the deuce is he talking about ? " demanded Iskander Beg of his companion.

" I don't know, but it seems to me that, speaking as he does of the past, the idiot thinks to regale us only with his wife's trousers."

" Why not ? " said Iskander; " they are greasy enough for that! "

Then, to the Tartar, —

" Tell us, now, friend, is there any chance of our having a dish of soup and a bit of chislik ?  Here is bread and cheese, it is true; but the bread is very moist and the cheese very dry."

" Soup ? And where should I get soup ? " answered Agraïne. " Chislik ? And where should I get chislik ? Khan Muel has eaten my sheep to the very last. Ah! my wife, my beautiful young Oumi, used to prepare such delicious chislik ! "

And the Tartar smacked his lips.

" And where is she, your young and beautiful Oumi ? " asked Yussef.

" She is dead and buried," replied the Tartar, " and I buried my last fifty roubles with her; I have nothing left of her but her trousers, over which I weep."

And, in fact, the Tartar took up the trousers, which he pressed to his lips, and fell to weeping.

" A precious souvenir," remarked Yussef. " She must have been a charming woman, your lovely young Oumi. Give us each a glass of milk and we will weep with you."

" Milk ? Oh! you should have seen my dear Oumi milking the cows with fingers whiter than the milk itself. But no more Oumi, no more cows; and no more cows, no more milk! and now — "

" Now you are beginning to weary us, my dear fellow, with your young and lovely Oumi. Fifty kopecks if you bring us each a glass of milk; if not, take yourself off."

And he thrust him out of the room.

" I will sell your mother for two onions, you villanous beast! " continued Yussef, returning to his seat near Iskander, and trying his teeth on the cheese. " All the cocks of the village are crowing in my stomach, and this scoundrel tries to entertain us with the trousers of his beautiful young Oumi. — Good! there he is now meddling with our guns and gossiping with the passers-by. — What do you mean by whispering to that vicious Lesghian, like a Schummak Bayadere, you wretched knave, instead of bringing us something to eat? So help me, Allah! but I am hungry enough to devour the fish that caused the universal flood by flopping from the Ganges into the sea. Come, bring us something, quickly!"

"Immediately," replied the Tartar.

And, indeed, he returned a few minutes later holding in each hand a bowl of milk.

Our travellers dipped their bread into the milk, while their host resumed his weeping where he had left off, again contemplating his wife's trousers.

Having ended their frugal repast, Yussef threw down sixty kopecks on the trousers of the beautiful young Oumi, and, leaping to their saddles and taking the mountain road, they had very soon left the village of Seyfouri behind.

"Look back now," bade Yussef, always on the alert, to Iskander. "The very Lesghian that the soft-hearted Agraine was talking to is keeping us in sight and watching where we go."

In fact, behind the two travellers, on a slight rise of ground, they could descry the interlocutor of the Tartar landlord.

But when the Lesghian discovered that he was himself an object of interest to the travellers, he disappeared.

"Well, what of it?" demanded Iskander.

"I distrust these beggarly Lesghians, — that is what!"

"According to you, every shepherd is a robber."

"As if shepherds were honest men in this country! The mountaineers murder travellers and pillage caravans, and the shepherds feed the mountaineers and receive their booty. Mullah Nour's entire troop, entire gang, rather, what is it? Made up of mountaineers. And who feeds Mullah Nour and his gang? The shepherds."

"Well, what then? Are not Mullah Nour and his mountaineers made of flesh and blood as we are? The devil take me if you do not make me wish to meet this bandit of yours, were it only out of curiosity, and to see whether, as you have said, his skin is proof against a ball."

"Well, well, here we are back on the old subject. You are either a dog or a pagan, however, to express such a wish. Does it seem, then, such a burden to carry your soul around in your body and a head on your shoulders? May the devil seize my nose if I would not rather meet a lion than this Mullah Nour. Why — why do you halt?"

"If you had not been in such a panic, you would not have lost your way. Look, pray, where you have brought us. The devil could not pass here without a lantern!"

And, indeed, the two found themselves upon a steep mountain, forming, so to speak, the first round of the ladder up Schach Dagh. Their way was becoming so perilous, that our travellers were obliged to dismount and lay hold of their horses' tails.

At length they reached a plateau, and, as usual, Yussef, who had maintained silence in the presence of danger, began as soon as the danger was over to curse and swear.

"May the devil's tail hack this mountain into mincemeat!" said he; "may all the wild boars of Daghestan root holes into it! may an earthquake upset it, and may thunderbolts grind it to powder, — curse it!"

"The fault is yours, and you lay the blame on the mountain," said Iskander, shrugging his shoulders. "What was it that you told me? 'I know the way as well as I know my mother's pockets; I will conduct you through the defiles of Schach Dagh as easily as I could make the rounds of the bazaar. I have played at hucklebones on every rock, and at pitch-penny in every cranny.' Did you or did you not say all that?"

"Certainly I said it. Did I not, three years ago, make the ascent of Schach Dagh's topmost peak? However, three years ago it was not so steep as now."

And, indeed, at the point where our travellers had now arrived, Schach Dagh rose before them, a sheer wall surmounted by white battlements; and the white battlements were snow.

The two men comprehended the impossibility of scaling the peak from that side.

They resolved to attempt the task from the east side. Yet it was easier to resolve than to execute. All was wild and lonely on those steep and rocky declivities; the eagles' cries alone broke the solemn stillness which seemed like that of the dead.

Iskander Beg turned toward Yussef and looked at him as if to say: "Well?"

"May a thousand million curses fall on the head of this miserable Schach Dagh! Ah! this is the way he receives his visitors, the ill-mannered pig! He pulls his bashlik over his ears, shuts himself within his walls, and hauls up his ladder after him. Where shall we go now? Over the mountain or under the mountain? I' faith, ask advice of whom you will, Iskander; as for me, I shall take counsel of my bottle."

And Yussef drew from his pocket a full flask of brandy.

"What a hardened sinner you are, you wretch!" exclaimed Iskander to his comrade. "Have you not enough folly of your own without adding that of wine?"

"This is not wine, it is brandy."

"Wine or brandy, it is all one."

"Not at all; observe the distinction: Mahomet has forbidden wine, but not brandy."

"I am aware of that; it was not invented in Mahomet's time: he could not forbid what did not exist."

"That is where you are wrong, Iskander. As a prophet, Mahomet knew very well that brandy would be invented later, or, if he did not know it, — why, he was a false prophet."

"No blasphemy, Yussef!" remonstrated Iskander, frowning; "let us seek, rather, our way."

"Our way? It is here," said Yussef, slapping his flask.

He approached the bottle to his lips, blissfully closed his eyes, and tossed off five or six swallows of the liquor whose orthodoxy was contested.

"Yussef, Yussef," said Iskander, "I can myself foretell one thing: with such a guide, you will more speedily attain hell than heaven."

"Well, what did I tell you, Iskander?" returned Yussef. "Before I had given that fraternal kiss to my flask, I could not see a single path; now, *brrruh!* I see a dozen of them."

"That may be, Hadji Yussef; I shall not follow your paths, however," said Iskander. "Take the right, take the left, take whichever you will; I shall attempt to climb straight ahead. If either of us finds a good way, he can return here and call the other, or wait for him. I shall take half an hour and give you as long for the quest. *Au revoir!*"

Hadji Yussef, animated by the five or six swallows of brandy that he had taken, deigned no reply to Iskander. He set out bravely to seek a path.

Iskander, therefore, leading his horse by the bridle, began to ascend straight ahead, as he had said.

The day was drawing near its close.

## VIII.

### HOW YUSSEF REACHED THE SUMMIT OF THE MOUNTAIN SOONER THAN HE WISHED.

DIRECTLY above the spot where the two travellers separated, near the border-line of clouds and snow, arose an enormous rock. On its flattened top men and horses found refuge.

Sixteen Tartars and one Lesghian were lying around a fire; as many horses as there were men were eating grass that had been mowed with poniards.

A few steps away, lying on a rug, was a man of about forty years, distinguished by the beauty of his countenance and its serenity of expression.

He was dressed very simply; yet — and this was indicative, not of wealth, but of the customs of a warlike life — gold and silver gleamed from his gunstock and from the sheath and blade of his kandjiar.

He was smoking a chibouk, and fondly regarding a sleeping youth, whose head was resting on his knees. At times he sighed, shaking his head, and again he would sigh heavily, casting an anxious glance around.

It was Mullah Nour, the scourge of Daghestan; the brigand, Mullah Nour, and his band.

Suddenly, a thousand feet below, he caught sight of Yussef, who, still seeking a path by which to scale the heights of Schach Dagh, was cautiously advancing amid he rocks

Mullah Nour, resting on his elbow, watched the traveller's movements a little while; then he smiled, and bending down to the youth's ear, he said, —

" Awake, Goulchade."

Goulchade, in Tartar speech, means *the rose.*

The youth opened his eyes, smiling also.

" Goulchade," said Mullah Nour, " would you like me to bow down to the earth before you ? "

" I should like it very well," said the young man, " and it would be a strange sight to see you at my feet."

" Softly, softly, Goulchade! Before the bee's honey is the sting. Look down there."

The young man lowered his gaze in the direction indicated by Mullah Nour.

" Do you see that traveller riding along ? "

" Of course I see him."

" I know his name and his courage. He is as fearless as a leopard; he is the best shot in Derbend. Go down, disarm him, and bring him to me. If you do that, I will be your slave the whole evening, and before all your comrades will I do you homage. Come, do you consent ? "

" Gladly," returned Goulchade.

And the young man leaped upon a wiry little mountain horse and set off by a narrow trail, which seemed rather a line traced with a crayon than a road channelled in the rock.

The stones could still be heard rolling from under his horse's hoofs, when the rider himself was no longer visible.

Mullah Nour's entire band peered over the rock, curious to see what would happen.

The chief was more intent than all the rest.

Perhaps he regretted that he had exposed the youth

to this danger; for, when Goulchade was but a few paces from Yussef, his chibouk fell from his hands, and anxiety was portrayed on his countenance.

Hadji Yussef had no idea of what was happening, or rather, of what was about to happen. Stimulated by the few swallows of brandy that he had taken, he was endeavoring to keep his courage up by talking aloud, and was putting on as bold a front as Shinderhannes or Jean Shogar.

"Oh! ho!" he was saying. "No, it is not for nothing that my gun bears the inscription: '*Beware! I breathe flame.*' I will burn the beard of the first bandit that dares to cross my path. Besides, I have nothing to fear; my breastplate is proof against bullets. But where are these brigands now? They are hiding, the cowards! Doubtless they can see me. Allah! for my part, I detest cowards!"

And suddenly, having reached a turn in the path, as the last syllable came thundering from his mouth, he heard a gruff voice cry out, —

"Halt! and dismount!"

And as he lifted his head in great dismay, he perceived, ten feet distant, the muzzle of a gun pointed at his breast.

"Come, come, down from your horse, and speedily!" was ordered a second time, in a tone that seemed gruffer than the first. "Make no attempt to put your hand to your gun or schaska! If you try to fly, I shall fire. The gun first!"

"Not only my gun, but my soul, master bandit," replied Yussef, quaking. "I am a good fellow, incapable of harming any one whatever. Don't kill me, and I will be your slave. I will take care of your horse and brush your clothes."

"Your gun! your gun!" repeated the voice.

"There it is," said Yussef, laying it down upon a rock with trembling hand.

"Your other arms, now,— schaska! kandjiar! pistol!"

"Here it is," faltered the unhappy Yussef at each item of the command, simultaneously casting on the ground the weapon designated by the bandit.

"Now turn your pockets."

Yussef flung all his money down beside the arms, imploring the bandit's mercy while executing his orders.

"I will cut off your tongue and throw it to the dogs if you do not hold your peace," said Goulchade. "Be silent, or I will silence you forever!"

"Excuse me, master bandit; I will not speak another word, if that is your desire."

"Silence, I tell you!"

"I hear and obey."

But not until Goulchade had pointed a pistol at Yussef did he cease to talk.

Goulchade bound his hands, took up his arms, and made him walk in the direction of the plateau where Mullah Nour and his comrades were awaiting the end of the comedy.

After a quarter of an hour's climbing, Yussef stood before the chief of the brigands.

His comrades formed a circle round him; all maintained an ominous silence.

Goulchade laid Yussef's weapons at the feet of Mullah Nour.

Then Mullah Nour saluted Goulchade three times, bowing down to the ground, and the third time, he kissed the youth's forehead.

Then turning to Yussef, he demanded, —

" Do you know who disarmed you, Yussef ? "

Yussef's whole frame shook at the sound of that voice.

" The bravest of the brave, the mightiest of the mighty!  How could I prevail against him, before whom a lion would become a hare, and Goliath be as a child but eight days old ? "

The bandits burst into laughter.

" Behold, then, the bravest of the brave, the mightiest of the mighty," said Mullah Nour, as he lifted the white papak from Goulchade's head.

And the long black locks fell down upon the shoulders of a girl, who became as pink as the flower whose name she bore.

Mullah Nour held open his arms to her, and she threw herself on the brigand's breast.

" Yussef," said Mullah Nour, " I have the honor to present my wife."

A wild burst of laughter greeted the ears of the unhappy prisoner.

He turned purple with shame, and yet, recovering himself, he said, —

" Do me a favor, master; do not sell me in the mountains.  I can pay you a noble ransom."

Mullah Nour's eyebrows drew together as black as two thunder-clouds.

" Do you know to whom you are offering a ransom, skin of a hare ? " he cried to Yussef.  " Think you, wretch, that I am a Derbend butcher that I should sell spoiled meat for fresh ?  Do you suppose that I would demand gold for you when you are not worth an ounce of lead ?  Why should I sell you in the mountains? Tailless dog that you are, what are you good for ?  Not even to root the earth with your nose.  You will tell me that you can, as well as any nurse or old governess, tell tales of ogres and giants to the little ones; but, for that, you must dress like a woman, and, instead of amusing the poor innocents, you would frighten them. Well, Yussef, you see that I know you; you see that I am not a flatterer. Now, do you in turn tell me what you think of me. I am Mullah Nour."

Upon hearing that terrible name, Hadji Yussef fell on his face to the earth, as if he had been struck by a thunderbolt.

" Allah! " said he, " you wish me to say what I think of you, how I regard you, — I who would be proud to perform my ablutions with the dust[1] of your feet? May Hussein and Ali preserve me! "

" Listen, Yussef," said Mullah Nour, " and bear this in mind: I have an abhorrence of giving the same command twice. I have asked you once what you think of me; I ask you a second time, but know that it is the last. I am listening."

" What do I think of you? May the devil crack my head like a nut, if I think anything of which you could complain. I, think ill of you? I, a cipher! I, a mere atom of dust! "

" Yussef," said Mullah Nour, stamping his foot, " I tell you that I have never repeated the same order thrice."

" Be not angry! be not angry, mighty Mullah Nour! Consume me not with the fire of your wrath. Your wish has transformed the ideas of my brain into pearls, but these pearls are mere glass in comparison with your endowments. What do I think of you, illustrious Mullah Nour? Well, since you insist, I will tell you.

[1] When water is not to be had, Mussulmans may perform their ablutions with dust or sand.

I think that your mind is a gun adorned with silver and gold; its charge is wisdom; it never misses fire and always hits the mark; I think that your heart is a flask of attar of roses, diffusing the perfume of your virtues on all around you; I think that your hand dispenses good broadcast, as the husbandman scatters grain; I deem your tongue a branch bearing flowers of justice and fruits of mercy. Even now I hear you say: ' Go home, my good Yussef, and remember Mullah Nour as long as you live.' Well, am I right, mighty man ? "

" It were nothing to say that you are a great orator. But you are a false seer, and, to prove that you have lied, here is my decision: Because you, a beg, allowed yourself to be disarmed, bound, and taken prisoner by a woman — "

" Is not Death herself a woman also," interrupted Yussef, " and more terrible than the most terrible of men ? "

" Let me finish, Yussef; I shall not be long. Since whoever is afraid of death is unworthy of life, you shall die."

Yussef gave a groan.

" To-morrow will be the last morning of your life, and if you say a single word, if you put forth a single plea, if you utter one complaint," added Mullah Nour, putting his hand to his poniard, " you will not even see to-morrow. Come, let him be more securely bound, let him be taken to the cave, and leave him there alone. There he can talk at will and as much as he pleases."

Mullah Nour gave the signal, and poor Yussef was picked up and carried off like a sack of meal.

" He will die of terror before to-morrow," said Goulchade to her lover. " Do not frighten him so, my beloved."

**6**

"Nonsense!" laughed Mullah Nour, "this will be a lesson for him; he will learn, the craven, that fear saves no one. The coward dies a hundred deaths; the brave man only one, and even then he goes to meet it."

Then, turning again to the bandits, he said, —

"My children, I am leaving you for an hour; if anything should happen to me, — if, by chance, I do not return, — well, Goulchade could lead you. She has proved to-day that she is worthy to command men. Ill betide him who does not obey her! Adieu, Goulchade," he added, straining the young woman to his heart and kissing her brow; "and I bid you adieu and embrace you because I anticipate an encounter somewhat more serious than yours. For a long time I have wished to measure my skill with Iskander Beg's, and, thanks to my noukar, I know where to find him. If I do not return before night, follow my trail in the mountains and endeavor to recover my body, that I may not be eaten by jackals, like a dead horse. If you hear shots and voices, let no one stir. If Iskander kills me, let no one avenge my death. Let the man that kills Mullah Nour be sacred to you, for he will be a brave man. I go in pursuit; adieu."

He slung his gun across his back and departed.

## IX.

### THE PRECIPICE.

MEANWHILE Iskander Beg had found a path that wound around the mountain.

On his right dropped a precipice; on his left arose walls furrowed at intervals as by thunderbolts.

But there was no return for the dauntless traveller; he needs must always advance. The way was too narrow for a horse to turn, and he went forward.

At last he came to an overhanging rock, under whose arch he must pass.

Beneath its vault the road was missing, but a block of ice, dislodged from the mountain, constituted a frail, transparent bridge.

Below this bridge, at the bottom of the abyss, thundered a torrent.

The young man halted; for an instant he paled, and the perspiration dampened his brow; but a thought of Kassime restored his self-possession.

Then his practised eye observed a horse's tracks on the ice; he pressed his own forward, urging him on with knees and voice. By crossing swiftly, the strain would be less.

Behind, he could hear the broken ice crashing into the gorge.

At last he began to breathe more freely, perceiving at the farther end of the tunnel the light's increasing brightness from the reflection of the snow.

But suddenly, enframed in the opening, appeared a horseman whom the optical effect rendered of gigantic proportions.

"Halt, and throw down your arms, or you're a dead man!" cried the horseman to Iskander; "I am Mullah Nour."

In his first surprise at the unlooked for apparition, Iskander had reined in his horse; but, upon hearing the name of Mullah Nour, one danger made him forget the other.

He spurred on his horse, and, detaching the gun from his shoulder, he said, —

"You are Mullah Nour? Well, out of my way, Mullah Nour! You see very well that there is not room here for two."

"Let God decide, then, who shall pass," said the brigand, aiming his pistol at the breast of Iskander, who was not more than ten paces distant. "Shoot first."

"Shoot yourself. I am not hiding behind my horse, am I?"

They stood thus for some seconds face to face, each with his weapon raised, and waiting for the other to fire.

Then the one lowered his pistol, the other his gun.

"Well, you are brave, Iskander," said Mullah Nour, "and no one deprives a brave man of his arms. Give me your horse, and go where you will."

"Take my arms first, and then you shall take my horse; but as long as I have a load for my gun, as long as the soul remains in my body, the hand of dishonor shall not touch my horse's bridle."

Mullah Nour smiled.

"I do not need your gun, nor your horse," said he; "I merely wish you to do my will. Not for the sake

of miserable plunder has Mullah Nour made himself a
chief of brigands, but because he is accustomed to command. Then ill befall him that obeys not his command.
I have many times heard you spoken of; often has your
courage been extolled to me, and now I see for myself
that you are brave, Iskander. But I did not cross your
path for nothing. We do not part until our swords
have crossed. That is my last word. Salute me; say,
offering your hand, ' Let us be friends,' and the way is
yours."

"Stay, this is my answer," said Iskander, carrying
his gun to his shoulder and pulling the trigger.

But no discharge followed; doubtless a drop of water
fallen from the arch had dampened the priming.

Enraged, Iskander swung back the gun, drew the
pistol from his belt, and fired.

The ball flattened against the silver cartridge-boxes
that ornamented Mullah Nour's tcherkesse.

The latter did not move; he folded his arms and
replied by a mocking laugh to Iskander's rage.

"Oh, that shall not save you, brigand!" cried
Iskander.

And, with schaska uplifted, he bore down upon
Mullah Nour.

Mullah Nour's sword flashed from its sheath with the
swiftness of lightning.

Iskander's blade whistled above the brigand's head,
and the stroke descended like the wrath of God.

Then, with a rending crash, the icy bridge broke
beneath the feet of the two combatants. Iskander's
horse had upreared just as his master's sword was
descending upon the head of Mullah Nour; but the
brigand was not touched.

He had fallen into the chasm.

Iskander Beg, thrown over backward, had seized hold of a projecting rock; he clung to it with double tenacity upon feeling that his horse was for some cause sinking from under him. The ice-bridge had become an inclined plane, and the horse was slipping down its steep descent.

The animal made a supreme effort, gathered his whole strength into his hams, and, impelled by their steely springs, he cleared the yawning space and landed on the other side of the gulf, streaming with sweat, and quivering with terror.

Fortunately, Iskander had disengaged his feet from the stirrups. Encumbered by the rider's weight, the horse could not have cleared the abyss. Behind him, under him, the ice-bridge was crashing with a frightful sound. The gulf roared, as with the greed of a tiger devouring its prey; then a deathlike silence succeeded.

Iskander hung from the arch.

Below him, uncovered by the rupture of the bed of ice, a rock jutted upward, presenting a surface of two or three feet. All around it floated space.

Iskander felt his arms grow numb, his sinews snap.

He knew that he could not long sustain himself in that position; if his hold loosened, he was lost in spite of himself.

He calculated the distance with the cool eye of a mountaineer, straightened his arms to diminish this distance by their entire length, and let himself drop vertically upon the rock.

He stood on this granite pedestal like a bronze statue of Volition.

He was saved, at least for the time being; but to avoid dizziness, he was obliged to close his eyes for an instant.

He was not long in opening them again to note his surroundings and seek an issue.

This rocky excrescence, if it may be so called, was sloping on the outer side, slippery, crumbling in places, and yet practicable to the foot of a mountaineer.

Clinging with hands and feet, Iskander succeeded in achieving a semi-circle around the immense column.

He then found that he was on the farther side of the ravine.

To go back by the way that he had just come was impossible.  It would have been like climbing a wall.

There remained, then, but the one recourse of descending to the foot of the precipice and then following the torrent until he should find a practicable path.

But Iskander Beg was tormented by one idea, — to learn what had become of Mullah Nour.

A brave man, after all, was Mullah Nour, out-and-out brigand that he was.  If he were merely hurt, he must receive assistance ; if dead, his body must be saved from the teeth of wild beasts.

For any one other than Iskander or a mountaineer born on the side of a precipice, such a descent would have been impossible.

Iskander undertook it.

The road, or rather the path, by which he had come with his horse, was cut off, as we have said, by a deep gorge spanned by the ice-bridge, which had broken from under the horses' feet.  He gained the steep side of the gash-like cleft and made its descent, aided by the projections of its rugged surface.

It took more than an hour to advance a quarter of a verst.

At last he reached the bottom; then only did he dare to look above his head.

Mullah Nour, falling from a height of five hundred feet perhaps, had crashed through several bridges of ice, superposed one above another, and had ended by plunging into a vast bed of snow, from which the torrent gushed as from a glacier.

This snow, without possessing the firmness of rock or ice, could yet sustain a man's weight.

Iskander ventured upon it, at the risk of being engulfed. Only a pale, wan light penetrated the cleft. It was gloomy and cold.

He soon saw, by the line through the broken bridges above his head, that he must be nearing the spot where Mullah Nour had fallen.

The fall of horse and rider had indented an immense funnel in the snow.

Iskander carefully lowered himself into it and found resistance under his feet.

He had come upon the horse, whose neck was broken.

He searched for the man and found an arm.  He drew the arm toward him, making the horse his vantage ground, and succeeded in drawing the body out of the snow in which it was buried.

Mullah Nour was like one dead, — his eyes were closed, he did not breathe.

However, no limb was broken; no serious wound was apparent. In accordance with the laws of gravity, the animal's fall had preceded the man's, clearing a path for him. The horse had saved the rider.

Iskander succeeded in loading the body upon his shoulders, in getting out of the snow-funnel, and gaining the bottom of the valley.

He rubbed Mullah Nour's face with his rough cloak; he slapped the palms of his hands and threw ice-cold water into his face.

Mullah Nour remained unconscious.

"Just wait," muttered Iskander; "if you are not dead, I know how to waken you."

He sat down, placed Mullah Nour's head upon one of his knees, loaded his pistol and fired beside his ear.

The report echoed like a clap of thunder.

Mullah Nour opened his eyes and moved a hand toward his kandjiar.

"Ah! I was sure of it!" murmured Iskander.

Mullah Nour's hand was unable to execute its design, and fell back at his side.

His eyes stared vacantly; his mouth essayed to articulate some sound, but his tongue would not obey.

At last he breathed a sigh; thought, returning to his brain, lighted up his eyes with the fire of intelligence. His gaze fixed itself upon Iskander; he recognized him, understood that to him he owed his life. With an effort he whispered, —

"Iskander Beg!"

"Ah!" said the latter, "this is very lucky. Yes, Iskander Beg, who is not willing that you shall die — do you understand? — because you are a brave man; because jackals and foxes are common, but lions are rare."

A tear sprang to the brigand's stern eye; he pressed Iskander's hand.

"After God," said he, "I owe you my life; to you, then, as to God, is due my eternal gratitude. It is not for my life that I thank you, but for your having endangered yours to save mine. Men have insulted, scorned, betrayed me; I owe them ill-will; I have paid them in hatred. Nature has endowed me with many wicked instincts; men have attributed to me more than nature gave; but neither my friends nor my enemies can accuse Mullah Nour of being an ingrate. Listen, Iskander," added the bandit, raising himself a little, "misfortune follows every one; possibly it may some day overtake you. My heart and hand are at your service, Iskander, — a heart and hand that fear nothing in the world. I would sell and cut off my head to save you. For the rest, you shall judge me by my deeds. Let us see now how much I am hurt."

The bandit tried to rise, and after a few attempts, he found himself upon his feet. He felt of his arms, first one and then the other; then his thighs, then his legs; took a few steps, unsteadily, it is true, but still a few steps.

"My head," said he, "is still a little light, but nothing is the matter with the rest of me, by my faith! Come, let us go! Allah has preserved me! it would seem that I am still necessary to his designs on earth."

"And now," asked Iskander, "how do we get out of here ? "

"You are putting me to it," said Mullah Nour; "but I am forced to say what is so hard for men to admit, — I do not know."

"Yet we cannot die of hunger here," said Iskander.

"Before dying of hunger, we would first eat my horse, then yours; for, as I was falling, although I could not see much, I saw him ready to follow me."

"No, fortunately," said Iskander, with a feeling of real joy, "my poor Karaback was saved. And hark! by Allah! he is neighing! "

Both turned in the direction of the neighing, and they saw the horse coming toward them, following the bed of the stream.

"On my faith," said Mullah Nour, "you were asking

how we should get out of here; your horse is answering us. He must be the devil if we cannot go up the way he came down."

Overjoyed, Iskander went to meet his horse. The latter, in turn, ran to his master as rapidly as the difficult road permitted.

When horse and master were side by side, the man put his arms around the animal's neck and kissed him as he would have kissed a friend. The horse whinnied with delight; the man wept for joy.

"There," said Mullah Nour, who had looked on with a smile, "now that the meeting is over, if you will ask your horse the way, nothing need detain us here any longer, it seems to me."

Iskander sent his horse ahead of them, as if he had been a dog, and doubtless the animal understood the service that was demanded of his intelligence, for he took the very route by which he had come.

After nearly a demi-verst, he stopped, scented the ground, cast a glance overhead, and, without hesitation, began to ascend the mountain.

On looking carefully, they discerned a narrow path, scarcely perceptible, worn by the wild goats when descending to drink at the torrent.

The horse went first.

"Follow my horse and lay hold of his tail, — I will not say in case your head grows giddy, but in case your legs fail."

But Mullah Nour shook his head.

"I am at home," he said; "the mountain is my domain. It is for me to do the honors of my house; go first."

Iskander followed his horse. At the end of half an hour's almost impossible climbing, they found them-

selves upon the path which the bandit had taken in
order to intercept Iskander.

Of course this path led to the platform where Mullah
Nour had left Goulchade and her companions.

The sun was just setting. Goulchade and the brigand's
comrades, not seeing him return within the time that
he had fixed, were on the point of starting out to search
for him.

Goulchade threw her arms about her lover's neck; his
comrades gathered round.

But Mullah Nour put Goulchade aside, waved back
his comrades, and made way for Iskander to enter within
the circle of joyous faces, which overclouded at sight of
him.

" This is my elder brother," said he to his fellows.
" From this time forth you owe him three things which
you have sworn to me, — love, respect, and obedience.
Wherever he shall meet one of you, he may command
you as I myself. Whoever shall render him a service,
however small, becomes my creditor, and shall have the
right to exact his price with usury. To the one who
does him a great service, I shall be beholden forever;
but if one of you shall harm a hair of his head, that
one shall never be safe from my vengeance, even at the
bottom of the sea, or within the tomb; I swear it, —
and may the devil claw out my tongue with his nails
if I do not keep my oath! Now let us sup."

A rug was spread and a scanty meal was served. The
anxiety felt by the bandits concerning the absence
of their chief had caused them to think little about
supper.

Goulchade, according to the custom of the Tartar
women, did not eat with her lover. She stood shyly
back, leaning against a rock.

Iskander noted her tearful sadness; he asked that she should have a place on the rug.

" It is just," said Mullah Nour; " this day Goulchade has been a man, and not a woman."

The supper ended, Iskander, moved by the beauty of the summer night, touched by the brotherly attentions lavished on him by Mullah Nour, could not retain the secret that filled his heart.    He told his love for Kassime.

" Oh! " he exclaimed, " if some time I could take wings like a bird, I would bring Kassime up to this height! I would show her all that makes me sad and ashamed to gaze upon alone, so beautiful it is! I should rejoice in her admiration, and when she would say, ' It is magnificent! ' I should press her to my heart, answering, ' It is beautiful, but you are more beautiful; you are better than anything in the world! I love you more than the mountain, more than the valley, more than the streams, more than the whole of Nature! ' See, Mullah Nour, how the earth, softly lighted by the moon, sleeps in the midst of Nature's myriad smiles. Well, I believe it to be sweeter still for man to fall asleep under the kisses of the woman he loves. You are very fortunate, Mullah Nour; you are as free as the wind.    The eagle lends you his wings to fly among the highest peaks.    You have a fearless consort; that does not surprise me, but I envy you."

Mullah Nour sadly shook his head as he listened to the young man speaking thus upon life's threshold.

" To every man his fate," he replied; " but mark me, Iskander, envy not mine, and especially follow not my example.    It is dangerous to live among men, but it is sad to live without them.    Their friendship is like the opium that intoxicates and puts to sleep; but, believe

me, it is bitter to live with their hatred.  It is not my
own will, it is fate that has thrust me outside of their
circle, Iskander.  A stream of blood separates us, and
it is no longer in my power to overleap it.  That liberty
is a gift from heaven, the most precious of all, I know
well; but the outlaw has no liberty, — he has but inde-
pendence.  True, I am lord of the mountain; true, I
am king of the plain; but my empire is peopled only
with wild beasts.  There was a time when I hated men,
when I scorned them; to-day, my soul is sick of scorn-
ing and hating.  I am feared, men tremble at my name;
the mother uses it to still her crying babe; but the
terror one inspires is but a plaything, of which, like
all others, he quickly tires.  Undoubtedly, there is a
joy in humiliating men, in mocking at all they boast,
in exposing their baseness by opening their whited
sepulchres.  It yields one a moment's pride; he feels
himself more criminal, yet less contemptible than others.
That feeling gladdens for an hour and saddens for a
month.  Man is wicked; but, after all, man is man's
brother.  Look about us, Iskander.  How vast are the
mountains! how green the forests! how rich the lands
of Daghestan! yet there is not a cave in the mountain,
not a tree in the forest, not a house in the plain where
I can rest my head and tell myself, ' Here you can sleep
tranquilly, Mullah Nour; here an enemy's ball will
not find you in your sleep; here you will not be bound
like a wild beast.'  Your cities are peopled and often
gorged with inhabitants; yet, rich or poor, every man
has his place, his own roof to shield him from the rain,
to shelter him from the cold.  As for me, my bourka
alone is my roof, my shelter, my cover.  The town will
not grant me even a bit of earth in which to lay my
bones.  Sorrow is like the wife of the kahn; she knows

how to tread on velvet carpets, but she must also know, like the goat, how to leap from rock to rock. Sorrow is my shadow, and, as you see, my shadow follows me even here."

"You have suffered much, Mullah Nour?" Iskander asked, deeply interested.

"Do not remind me of it, friend. When you pass the gorge into whose depths I fell, and from which you rescued me, do not ask whether it was lightning or frost that ploughed the chasm in the granite, but pass over quickly; the bridge is frail and may give way beneath you. Flowers are planted in gardens, but the dead are not buried there. No, I will not cast a gloom over the morning with the storms of noon-tide. The past is past; it cannot be changed, even by the will of Allah. Good-night, Iskander. And God grant that no one may dream what I have suffered in reality. I will show you to-morrow the shortest way to reach Schach Dagh. Good-night!"

And he lay down, wrapped in his bourka; the others had been asleep for an hour.

Iskander waited long for sleep to come; he thought much of the day's events and Mullah Nour's solemn words.

Then, once asleep, he was troubled with the most fearful dreams. Sometimes it seemed as if a ball were piercing his heart, sometimes as if he were falling into a bottomless abyss.

Our dreams are but memories of the way we have come, — the confusion and excitement of past events.

There is but one dreamless sleep, — the deep sleep, death.

## X.

IN WHICH YUSSEF RELATES WHAT DID NOT HAPPEN,
BUT TAKES GOOD CARE NOT TO RELATE WHAT DID
HAPPEN.

THE sun, tinting the mountain-tops, awoke Mullah
Nour and his men. All first prostrated themselves in
prayer, then they set about polishing their arms, curry-
ing their horses, and preparing breakfast.

" Your travelling companion spent a bad night,"
announced Mullah Nour to his guest, with a laugh.

" What! Yussef?" inquired the latter.

" Yussef in person."

" You know where he is, then?"

" I have an idea."

" I begged you twice yesterday to have him searched
for, but you gave me no answer."

" Because I knew where to find him."

" And where is he?"

" Fifty paces from here."

" What do you intend to do with him?"

" Nothing at all. I give him to you; you may do
what you like with him. Eh! my lads," continued
Mullah Nour, addressing his men, " carry our prisoner
something to eat, and say that Mullah Nour does not
wish to starve him to death."

Then he told Iskander how Goulchade had stopped
Yussef, forced him to surrender his arms, and brought
him back with her as a prisoner.

When breakfast was over, Mullah Nour took Iskander by the hand and held him to his heart, and cheek to cheek.

" You are at home here," said he; " I shall always greet you with joy, I shall always love you with gratitude. Now I have pointed out a route by which you can ascend Schach Dagh, and the one by which you are to descend; make haste to serve your fellow countrymen. I myself am going in the opposite direction and for another purpose. Adieu! remember Mullah Nour; if you are in need of a friend, summon him, and the avalanche will not more swiftly reach the mountain's foot than he will reach you."

And, like a flight of wild pigeons, the chief and all his band whirled out of sight.

Iskander then went to the cave.

Yussef was lying down with his hands tied, his eyes bandaged.

The young beg could not resist the desire to experiment on the courage of his companion.

" Get up, and prepare to die! " said he, roughly, disguising his voice.

Yussef trembled in every limb; but, thanks to a strenuous effort, he managed to get upon his knees.

He was deathly pale; his nose seemed to have lost that firm base by whose help it ordinarily formed an acute angle with his mouth, an obtuse angle with his chin, and drooped inert over his lips. He raised his hands to heaven and implored pardon between his groans.

" O Angel Azraël," he cried, " spare my head, it is not ripe for death! Where and how have I offended you ? "

" It is not my will, it is Mullah Nour's. He said:

7

' Yussef fought like a tiger; now that Yussef knows my retreat, there is no more safety for me in the mountain. Besides, the blood of my comrades spilled by him at the siege of Derbend cries aloud for vengeance, and it must be taken.' "

" I! " cried Yussef, " I! I fought in the siege of Derbend ?   What abominable calumniator says that ?   Shame befall the tomb of his fathers and of his grandfathers, even to the tenth generation!  No, no!  I am not the man to fight against my compatriots, not I.    When trumpet or drum called to the rampart, for my part I descended at once to the bazaar; and when it was my turn to march, I took refuge in the mosque and slept there honestly and conscientiously, to the glory of the prophet.   True, one day I fired three shots; but it is an established fact that the enemy was five versts away. As for my sabre, try yourself to draw it, and if you can get the blade out of its sheath, you may strike off my head with it.   Not once, since the days of my father, has it ever been out.   And why should I have fought against Kasi Mullah, against a brave, a holy man, a prophet ?   Had he not cut off the heads of all who drank and smoked, I should be to-day one of his most ardent fanatics."

" That may be; but there is a religious side to Mullah Nour's wrath against you; he knows that you are a partisan of Ali, and he has sworn to slay all who believe in Ali."

" A partisan of Ali, I ?   Why, I would pluck him by the beard, this Ali and his twelve caliphs!   What is more, if I had lived in Egypt in the time of the Fatimites, I should not have rested until I had dragged them from the throne.   I am a Sunnite, pray understand. a Sunnite. heart and soul !  Who is he. this Ali ?

An atom of dust, — I give a puff and it flies away; a grain of sand, — I crush it under foot as I walk."

"But, above all, look you, the thing Mullah Nour will never forgive you is your friendship for Iskander, his mortal enemy."

"My friendship!" cried Yussef.

"Was it not a proof of friendliness, then, your accompanying him to Schach Dagh?"

"Of friendliness, no doubt, directed especially toward my own pleasure."

"Well, the affair has ended rather worse for him than for you, and his head has fallen before yours."

"His head has fallen?" echoed Yussef.  "Ah, well, it was no great loss, that.  His head was not of much account.  But instead of bearing me ill-will, Mullah Nour ought to thank me, since it was I who brought him Iskander, who delivered him up, bound hand and foot.  Iskander my friend?  A precious friend he is now! but when he was alive, I would have exchanged him for a piece of gingerbread.  Iskander my friend! one of the greatest rakes in Derbend, who ate ham with the Russian officers?  He my friend?  I would burn his mother's beard."

"Wretch that you are!  Leave the dead in peace. If fear had not turned your head, you would reflect that his mother could n't have a beard."

"No beard?  Why, I tell you, myself, that she used to shave.  Allah! the number of razors that she broke! Iskander's friend?  I? — why, would I have been such a fool as to make a friend of a man whose father was a brigand, whose mother was a lunatic, and whose uncle made boots?"

"I am tired of hearing you perjure yourself, renegade! liar! tongue of a dog!  Bend your neck, the sword is raised!"

Iskander made his schaska whistle around Yussef's head; but instead of touching him with its blade, with his usual skill he lifted on its point the handkerchief that bandaged his eyes.

Yussef, terror-stricken, looked at his pretended executioner and recognized skander.

He uttered a cry and sat stupefied.

" Well, and what do you see, you wild boar stuffed with folly ? Come, tell me again that my father was a brigand, my mother was a lunatic, and my uncle made boots! "

Yussef, instead of seeking pardon and looking confused, burst out laughing, and threw himself upon Iskander's neck.

" Ah! then I have managed to put you in a rage. There was no lack of skill on my part. It took a long time, but I succeeded at last. Ha! ha! snare a nightingale, and catch a crow! Why, do you think that, with the very first word, I did not recognize your voice, — your voice, the voice of my best friend ? Why, I should know it amidst the crying of jackals, the miauling of cats, and the barking of dogs! "

" Very well; you knew me? "

" Do you doubt it ? "

" No; you scoffed at me. "

" Just for a laugh, a joke, — for nothing else; you understand, surely ? "

" But how about your surrendering to Mullah Nour's wife ? How about your letting her disarm you ? "

" Do you not recall having seen at the house of the commandant of Derbend an engraving which represents a very beautiful woman indeed, unlacing the breastplate of a beg called Mars ? Underneath, it says in Russian: *Mars disarmed by Venus.* That is the reason why I allowed myself to be disarmed, my dear friend. Why, to such a beautiful creature I would have given up everything, Iskander, from my bourka to my heart. I would like to know what you would have done, you rogue, on meeting her face to face. Such a nose! such eyes! and a mouth no bigger than the hole in a pearl bead! And her figure, too! A connoisseur like you would have noticed her figure. I longed to rob her of her belt to make me a ring."

"And so it was for love that you let yourself be bound, and that is why you followed her at the end of a rope?"

"I would have followed her at the end of a hair."

"Perhaps; yet one thing is very certain, — you will not talk in Derbend, and especially in my presence, of your devotion to Goulchade."

"Goulchade? Her name is Goulchade? What a charming name! But you are the one that is making me prate; that is the reason why I have not asked how you chance to be here."

Iskander briefly related what had passed between him and Mullah Nour. When he reached the point of the brigand's fall over the precipice, Yussef interrupted him.

"Then he must be dead?" said he.

"No."

"What! not dead?"

Iskander told how he had saved Mullah Nour and returned him to his men.

"Then he is there, this dear Mullah Nour?" demanded Yussef.

"No, he has gone away."

"Where?"

"On an expedition."

" You are very sure of it ? "

" I have seen the dust flying after his last horseman."

" And he fell from a height of five hundred feet, say you, and the devil did not break his neck ? and he did not shatter his arms and legs into a thousand pieces? I shall spit on the gun of that brigand yet. Ah! if he had come to bar my way himself, instead of sending his wife, I should have taught him how to write the word *brave*. But he did not dare, the coward ! "

" Come, come, be silent, you braggart ! Why, if you had met Mullah Nour in person, you would have left off lying and boasting, for you would have been frightened to death."

" Frightened ! I ? Learn, my dear Iskander, that there is but one man in the whole world that can make me afraid, and he is the man I see in the mirror when I look at myself."

This time Iskander could not contain himself. The gasconade was so strong, even for a Tartar, that he burst out laughing.

" Come," said he, " enough of this. You have just taught me something new about yourself, and yet I thought I knew you very well. To horse ! and away, brave Yussef! "

" You know the road ? "

" Yes; Mullah Nour pointed it out to me."

" Well, go ahead and I will follow you, and he shall fare ill that attacks us in the rear."

Iskander took the path which the bandit had shown him.

Watching them from below, one would certainly not have thought that human beings would venture on such a road.

When they had reached the snow line. Iskander gave

his horse to Yussef to hold, and he alone, jar in hand, began to scale the highest peak.

For the first time, this virginal snow was receiving the imprint of a human foot.

Iskander prostrated himself upon the peak where, hitherto, only the angels had prayed.

When he lifted his head and gazed about, he looked upon a land of marvellous beauty.

Before him ran down the whole chain of mountains which extend from the Caspian Sea to the Avari; his sight penetrated the depth of the valleys, where he saw rivers as shining and slender as silken threads.

All was calm and silent. Iskander was too far distant to be able to distinguish either men or animals; too high up to hear a sound.

He might have remained a long time admiring the splendid spectacle, had not the atmosphere, totally free at this height from all terrestrial vapors, been too rare for human lungs.

The young beg's every artery began to throb, as if the blood, not being sufficiently compressed by the air, were ready to issue from the pores.

He then bethought him to acquit himself of his mission, and in his profound faith that everything was possible to the God between whom and himself nothing seemed to intervene, he formed a ball of snow, placed it in his vase, and began to descend, holding the vessel high above his head, in order that, in accordance with the decree, it should not be sullied by contact with the earth.

The descent was as difficult as the ascent, in a very different way; but throughout the entire expedition, a higher power had seemed to watch over Iskander.

At the end of almost an hour he found himself beside Yussef.

Yussef questioned him, but Iskander shook his head.

Yussef tried to engage him in jest, but Iskander gravely pointed to the sky.

He was descending to the plain, full of the sublimity of those tall summits.

"Umph!" said Yussef, "you must have taken a bite of the sun up there; you seem afraid of dropping a morsel if you open your mouth."

But Yussef spoke in vain; he did not succeed in extracting a single word from Iskander.

He finally became silent in turn.

In spite of all their haste, our travellers did not arrive at Derbend until far into the night, and long after the gates had been shut.

Iskander's heart beat as if it would rend his breast; fear, doubt, hope, challenged each other with every throb. He hung the jar on a branch of a tree, and moodily regarded, sometimes the black wall, which separated him from what he held dearest on earth, sometimes the heavens, which seemed to be frowning at him. He appeared to be asking all Nature: "Must I fear? May I hope?"

Ere long he saw with joy that clouds were gathering in the sky and stealing over the brilliant face of the moon.

Overjoyed, he plucked the sleeping Yussef by the arm and exclaimed, —

"Look, Yussef! look at these clouds scudding across the heavens, hurrying like a flock of sheep!"

"A flock of sheep!" muttered Yussef. "Pick out the tenderest, and take the ramrod from my gun to make chislik out of him. I am literally dying of hunger."

"Listen to the animal," said Iskander; "he never thinks of anything but his stomach. The sheep that I am talking about are in the clouds, Yussef; it is going to rain, my friend."

"Ah!" murmured Yussef, "if that meant larks, I would get under the spout, with my mouth wide open, too!"

"Well, sleep then, brute, for there is a proverb that says: 'Who sleeps, dines.'"

"Good-night, Iskander!" said Yussef, yawning.

And he went to sleep on his bourka. As for Iskander, he did not close his eyes during the night, nor did he cease scanning the heavens, which became more and more overcast.

At daybreak the gates of Derbend were opened, and in a brief space of time it was known throughout the town that Iskander had arrived with the snow from Schach Dagh.

After a short prayer, the mullahs, accompanied by the people, led the way to the sea.

Iskander modestly bore the vessel containing the melted snow; but Yussef, the centre of an immense crowd, narrated with great gusto the events of their journey. Only, in Yussef's story, Iskander wholly disappeared. As for himself, Yussef, he had gone so near to heaven as to hear the snoring of the seven sleepers and the voices of the houris. He had suffered horribly from the cold; but, fortunately, he had got warmed up in a fight with two bears and a serpent of frightful dimensions. He had wished to bring home the serpent's skin, and had flayed it for that purpose; but his horse was so terribly afraid of it that he was obliged to abandon it on the way. However, he knew exactly where it lay, and, on the morrow, he would send the muezzin to fetch it.

But, however interesting Yussef's tales might be, he

had not a single auditor when the time came for Iskander
to turn the water from his jar into the sea.

Since early morning a high wind had been blowing;
but the wind brought no rain,— not one drop of water
fell.

When, after a long prayer by the mullah, Iskander
was ready to empty his jar into the Caspian, he turned
to Festahli, who was walking in the front rank, and
said, —

" Remember your promise."

" Remember the conditions," Festahli in turn replied.
" Your fate lies not with the snow, but with the rain.
If you are dear to Allah, you are very dear to me."

Iskander elevated the jar above his head, and in the
sight of all he poured the snow-water from Schach Dagh
into the sea.

Immediately, as if by magic, a great tempest arose;
clouds, which seemed charged with rain, blackened
the sky; thunder was heard rumbling in the distance;
the leaves, violently agitated by the wind, shook off the
dust which covered them.    Young Tartar girls peeped
brightly from the veils which the wind tried to snatch
from their heads.    The hands of all were outstretched
to feel the first drops of the rain so impatiently awaited.
At last a flash rent the dome of clouds amassed above
Derbend, and it seemed as if all the windows of heaven
had opened at once in another deluge.

A torrent of rain poured from the clouds and flooded
the land of Daghestan.

This time no one dreamed of fleeing, no one thought
even of opening his umbrella.

Not joy, but delirium, possessed the people.

Papaks flew up into the air and fell back into the
water; prayers and shrieks of delight joined in flight to

heaven.   They hugged each other, they congratulated each other, they gazed at the water which was descending like a giant waterfall, or rather, like a hundred waterfalls, from Tartar city to Russian city, and leaping from the citadel into the sea.

Iskander alone felt more joy within himself than all the other inhabitants of Derbend put together.

For him, a wife was coming down from heaven with the rain.

## XI.

### TWO HOLY MEN.

YOUTH — what is it without love?  Love — what is it without youth?

The fire burns readily in pure air, and what air is purer than the breath of spring?

True, the walls of Mussulmans' courts are high, and the locks of their gates are strong; but the wind blows over the walls and through the key-holes.

The hearts of beautiful women are well protected, — they are kept behind the padlocks of a thousand prejudices; but love is like the wind, — it easily finds a passage.

Kassime was already in love without the courage to confess it.  Iskander Beg had the most of her thoughts by day and the most of her dreams by night; while embroidering in advance with gold, as every young Tartar girl does, the pistol-case for the *fiancé* whom she did not know, Kassime kept saying to herself, —

"Oh! if this might be Iskander's!"

Judge, then, of her joy when her uncle came officially to announce that she was the promised bride of this handsome young man!

She became redder than a cherry, and her heart began to beat like a wild dove's.

And so her dearest and most secret wishes were to be realized.

From that moment, her nameless hopes were called Iskander; from that moment she could receive with pride the congratulations of her companions, and, in her conversations with them, she, too, could speak of her future husband.

As for Iskander, he did not feel the earth under his feet, and to console himself for not being allowed to see his promised bride, he thought of her incessantly.

"She will work here on this rug; she will drink out of this cup; she will refresh her rosy cheeks with the water from this silver ewer; she will sleep under this satin coverlet."

Into those countries of the Caucasus that follow the religion of Ali, there frequently come priests and mullahs from Persia to expound the Koran and recount the miracles of their imáms.

This, as a rule, takes place in the month of May.

Beginning with the first day of this month, the Shiites celebrate the death of Hussein, Ali's son, who, after the death of his father, rebelled against Yazíd, son of Moawyah, with the intention of seizing the caliphate; but engaging in battle with Obaid Allah, Yazíd's general, he was killed in the combat. The Shiites celebrate the anniversary of this event with great splendor. The fête takes place at night, by the light of numberless torches; and this time, coming from Tabbas to direct the fête, Mullah Sédek had remained in Derbend throughout the entire month of May.

Mullah Sédek was a man of forty years, affecting extreme dignity, for which reason he walked as slowly as a man of seventy, — in a word, for twenty paces round him he exhaled the odor of sanctity and attar of rose.

And yet, while Sédek's eyes were raised to heaven, he never quite lost sight of earth. He had few friends:

but as soon as a man came to him with money in his hand, that man found a welcome. He had reaped a rich harvest of presents at Derbend, but it was his desire to carry away something else besides money and jewels. He thought of marrying, and after having secured information as to the best matches in the city, he made overtures to Hadji Festahli, with respect to his niece, whom he knew to be richly endowed.

He began his overtures by flattering Hadji Festahli, and as vanity was the weakness of Kassime's uncle, Sédek had, in a short time, come to be his most intimate friend.

" Ah," said Sédek, " the end of the world is not far distant now. Houtte, the fish on whose back the universe rests, is weary of bearing, along with the weight of men, the otherwise heavy burden of their sins. The Mussulmans are corrupt: they worship money; they wear decorations in their button-holes and ribbons of many colors on their swords. Truly, I know not what would have become of Derbend when she was threatened by the Lord, if you had not been there to act with your virtues as a counterpoise to the crimes of the people. You are a pure man, a respectable man, a holy man, a true Shiite; you are in league with neither the Armenians nor the Russians. The only thing I will not and cannot believe is that you are marrying your niece to this wretched Iskander, who is as poor as a dervish's dog. When I heard that report I said to myself: ' It is not possible! A man like Hadji Festahli would not cast the pearl of the prophet into the mud; he will not give his brother's daughter to the first-comer.' No, I am sure it is either a lie or a jest."

" And yet, it is the truth," admitted Festahli, quite emlarrassed.

And he told Sédek the whole story; how Iskander had made his conditions, and how he himself had been obliged to consent to this marriage.

"I can say with truth," he added, "that there are in Derbend no eligible young men with fortunes; the rich men, as if by a curse, are all old."

Mullah Sédek stroked his beard and said: "All is from Allah! all shall return to Allah! Are there no true worshippers of Hussein in the land of Iran? The sun rises and sets twice each day in the great king's empire, and there is where you should choose a husband for your niece. O holy prophet, if you would mate the moon with one of the most glorious stars of heaven, I will send you my nephew, Mir Heroulah Tebris. He is intelligent and handsome; he is so rich that he does not know the number of his pearls and diamonds, and yet he is as shy and modest as a girl. When he passes through the bazaar, every one bows, and it is who shall provide him with fruits, with cakes, with raisins. There is no danger of a single visitor's presenting himself at his house without a present. If ever your niece becomes his wife, you can rest assured that she will have the first place in the baths of Tabbas."

This proposition was all the more pleasing to Festahli as it must destroy the hopes of Iskander, whom he could not endure.

However, he had scruples against thus breaking a sacred promise.

He therefore told Sédek that if such a transaction could be brought about, he would be rendered the proudest and happiest man in the world; but it was to be feared that Kassime's mother might not approve. Then, too, the commandant of Derbend would certainly not permit a native of his own town, and consequently a

Russian, to wed a Persian.  And, besides, what would
the people of Derbend say?

" *What will people say?* " has some weight in Paris
or at Saint Petersburg; but on the shores of the Caspian
Sea, in the Orient, it is an afterthought of one who has
forgotten his first.

" ' What will they say? ' " replied Sédek, banteringly.
" Why, they will say that you are a man of judgment!
To commit faults is pardonable, — to repair them, praise-
worthy; and, to be frank, what has this Iskander done
that is so wonderful?  Do you really believe that his
snow brought the rain?  Let me manage the thing, and
I will show you how this affair can be arranged.  In
the meantime, give out that your sister is dangerously
ill, and that, in fear of death, she has sworn to marry
her daughter to none but a descendant of the prophet,
to an imám.  Your sister never leaves her room; in
her room, even, she is as dumb as a fish: do not consult
her.  Have you not read in the sacred books how Job
beat his wife when she counselled him to make friends
with the devil?  Besides, is Kassime's mother your
wife?  What is she to you?  A sister; that is all.
Then spit upon her caprices."

" And the commandant? " said Festahli, smiling.

" What can the commandant do?  And then, cannot
the commandant be tricked?  What hinders your getting
a passport to go to see your relatives in Persia? "

Festahli consented, or rather, he had already consented long before.

The next day they sent back to Iskander the *kalmi*,
or wedding-present, which he had already given to his
betrothed.

The young man, not being able to tear his hair, very
nearly tore off his ears.  For a long time he could not

believe in this insult. But the bag, with the money it contained, was certainly there, under his very eyes. The old aunt could make nothing of it, and she pitied him with all her soul.

Iskander was overwhelmed.

He reviewed in his mind every means of avenging himself on Festahli without breaking the Russian laws. Ah! if there had been a khan at Derbend instead of a colonel! One thrust of a dagger, all would have been said, and Kassime would be his own.

But he must not think of such a measure, expeditious though it was.

Iskander became moody, and spoke no more than a dead man. He did not see Hadji Yussef, who had been standing in front of him a long time.

Apart from his cowardice and lying, Hadji Yussef was truly an excellent man. He was really moved by his friend's grief; he would have wept, had he known how.

"Why, what is the matter, my dear Iskander?" he asked.

"What is the matter yourself? what do you want of me?" demanded Iskander, frowning.

"I came to tell you that three vessels loaded with grain have arrived, and the people are well pleased. It is good news, Iskander."

"If you had come to tell me that three vessels loaded with poison had arrived, the news would be better still."

"Oh! oh! it is cloudy weather, is it? Come, tell me what vexes you."

"Why should I tell you? As if you did not know already. As if all Derbend did not know, for that matter."

8

" Is it true that Kassime's mother refuses you for a son-in-law ? "

" Her mother ? "

Iskander burst into a laugh that made Yussef shiver.

" Her mother ?   No; it is that wretch, Festahli," said he; " but I will kill him! "

" It is easily seen that you have eaten bread on the mountains, my poor Iskander.   It is not difficult to kill a man and run away; but, to the end of life, all thought of returning to one's native town must be given up. For my part, I advise you to content yourself with a good drubbing; afterwards, you can tranquilly retire to Baku.   If you absolutely wish to take a wife, well, you can get married there for three months; it will cost you twenty-five roubles.   It is a magnificent invention, especially for travellers, that sort of marriage.   I have tried it.   I was married one day, just as I am, for six weeks only.   I lacked the patience to serve out my time; I ran away at the end of a month.   When asleep, I was in constant fear lest my wife should bite off my nose, she was so crabbed and spiteful.   Try it, and I will wager that on your return you will bring me a present by way of thanks."

Iskander continued pensive and silent.

" My dear heart, my handsome lily, my proud palm, Iskander," resumed Hadji Yussef, " do you not hear me ? are your ears full of water ?   A bride! i' faith, a little matter that, a bride!   Take a handful of roubles, go and show them in the Derbend market, crying, ' A bride! a bride! ' and brides will flock around you like chickens."

Iskander still maintained silence.

" But what is there about it, then, to grieve you so, ʼskander.   The devil! that Kassime of yours is no star.

In the first place, one of her eyes is larger than the other, and then she is so black that she will ruin you in the one item of Spanish white. I can even add that she is slightly hump-backed. Don't contradict me, I know her, I have seen her."

Iskander heard this time; he seized Yussef by the throat.

"You have seen her! Where have you seen her? how did you see her? when? in what place did you dare raise your basilisk eyes to her? Why don't you answer me, wretch?"

"How can I answer you? you are choking me! Oh! in Allah's name, let me go! Can't you see that I am joking? You know very well that I keep my eyes in my pockets, and my pockets have no holes, thank God! And when could I have seen her, why should I have looked at her? Do I not know that she is the promised bride of my best friend? Never marry, Iskander; you are really too jealous for a man that is on good terms with the Russians. You would be obliged to stand guard all night, and to spy all day upon those who came to visit you. For that matter, I cannot see how they manage, these devils of Russians; they are not in the city ten days before they have already made friends with every one of our beauties. You know Mullah Kasim? — bless God; but he is jealous, that fellow; well, he bought himself a charming wife. As he had paid dearly enough for her, he determined to keep her to himself. His wife had but one friend in the world, — a woman could not have less. Three times a week the friend came to Mullah Kasim's house; he himself conducted her to his wife and stood guard at the gate, lest the two women should come upon the balcony and look down into the street. Do you know who that friend was? It was a young Russian ensign who had as yet no beard."

Iskander clutched Yussef's arm, but not in anger this time.

"A man dressed as a woman?" said he. "Yes, that might really be possible indeed. Thanks for your story, Yussef; it is very amusing."

"That is right. Well, now that you are in a better humor, I will leave you. I have a heap of business. This evening I represent the French ambassador at Yazíd's court. I must try on my tight trousers; I am afraid I shall not be able to get into them. May the devil make himself a jacket of a Russian's skin for having thought of inventing these damned pantaloons! Now, if I meet a cock, he may as well stand still, — I shall get his tail for a plume. You will see, Iskander, how haughty I shall be when I appear on the scene. Every soldier greets me with: ' We hope you are in good health, your Highness.' Adieu! I have no time to lose if I wish to be admitted."

And Yussef departed, throwing the sleeves of his tchouka back over his shoulders, that he might walk the faster.

Iskander sat alone, pensive, but smiling in his revery. The anecdote related by Yussef had given rise, in the midst of his garrulity, to an idea which was nothing less than to take advantage of the fête which they were then celebrating, — a kind of Mussulman carnival, — to disguise himself as a woman and approach Kassime.

Let us say forthwith that nothing adapts itself to such a disguise more readily than the Tartar costume, with its wide trousers, arkalouke, and immense veil.

After he had decided upon this step, Iskander ceased to despair.

"Ah, I shall see her," said he, "and she shall be mine! Then, Festahli, you shall know what it means to awaken a tiger. Kassime, Kassime, expect Iskander, even if the road between us were paved with daggers!"

And, on the instant, Iskander set off for the bazaar, and purchased a woman's complete costume, pretending that it was a present for his *fiancée*.

Returning home, he despatched his noukar, whose indiscretion he feared, to the meadow with the horses; then, as soon as the noukar was gone, he shaved off all his beard, which, for the matter of that was barely beginning to grow; he stained his eyelids, painted his brows, put on some rouge and donned the trousers, arkalouke and veil; he practised the gait of the Tartar women in his new costume, retaining his bechemette so that he might be in masculine attire in case of necessity for attack or defence.

He awaited the evening impatiently; but the day, like a rich uncle, could not make up its mind to die.

At last, the gong beat for prayer, and the theatre was lighted.

Then Iskander placed on his cheeks two indispensable little spangles of gold, slipped his kandjiar into his girdle on one side and his pistol on the other, enveloped himself from head to foot in an immense white veil, and set out, carrying a little lantern in his hand.

At the end of a quarter of an hour, Kassime issued forth with two friends; all three were on their way to see the religious drama which was being enacted at Derbend in honor of the death of Hussein, and which very much resembles the Mysteries which the Brothers of the Passion used to perform in France during the Middle Ages.

Both streets and public squares were full of people

afoot and on horses; for it is remarkable that at out-of-door performances in the Orient, no matter how crowded the spectators may be, at least a third of them is on horseback. This third circulates about, goes and comes without concerning itself as to the feet it crushes or the shoulders it injures. It is the pedestrian's business to get out of the way and take care of himself. His only due is the Circassian warning, " *Kabarda! karbarda!* " uttered from time to time, and equivalent to our own " look out, there! "

The house-tops, the only points inaccessible to the horsemen, were covered with women enveloped in long veils of every color.

The play had not yet begun. Upon the stage fitted up for the presentation of " Yazíd," the name of the tragedy, Mullah Sédek, between two other Mussulmans, was reading the prologue, and, at the pathetic places, he interrupted himself to cry to the spectators, " Weep and wail, O ye people! " The people responded to the apostrophe with groans and lamentations.

Utterly reckless, Iskander, who had followed Kassime, climbed after her up the small staircase which led them to the roof of a house which was already covered by a throng of Moslem women irradiated by numerous torches.

The women embraced as they met and recognized each other, laughing and talking with ceaseless babble.

All were richly dressed, and adorned with gold and silver necklaces, and each exhibited to the others, as rival to rival rather than as friend to friend, the finery which she was wearing for the first time.

One who has had no experience of the Asiatic woman does not know, and never will know, the half of an Asiatic man, should he live with him many years. In the presence of unbelievers, the followers of the prophet

eternally wear a mask, and, outside of the harem, the
Oriental man never shows to his own brother either the
bottom of his heart or the depths of his purse. All
nations have the same ruling passion, — that of vaunt-
ing their own customs. The Mussulmans are addicted
to this more than any other people. If their word is
to be accepted, you can regard them every one as saints.
According to them, husbands and wives in the performance of their duties walk between the lines of the Koran
and never step aside either to right or left. Only within
his home does the Mussulman show himself as he is;
it is because he has to render no account of his conduct to either wife or children. The wife, contrariwise,
is quite free in her husband's absence. No sooner has
she seen the heels of his slippers, than she becomes unrecognizable. Speechless and humble before him, she
becomes garrulous, boastful, shameless even before her
female companions, with whom she is always sincere,
as jealousy exists among the women of the Orient only
in matters of costliness of apparel and value of gems.

Hence arises a double life entirely foreign to that of
Europe, whose nature this book will be at least one of
the first to signalize and impress, — a life less accessible
even to men than to women, because man constantly
reveals himself to woman, woman to man, never.

Now, suppose that in some way, — what way? that is
not my affair, — suppose that in some way you are in
the company of a Moslem woman; suppose that you
have penetrated to the bath and listened to her prattle
with a friend; that you have entered the harem and
seen her romp — it is the only word that presents itself
to my pen — romp, I say, with her companions; clearly,
you will learn more yourself than a Mussulman would
ever tell you, more than he himself will know.

Judge, then, of Iskander's astonishment when he found himself surrounded by feminine indiscretions. Lost in a flock of young women, pretty and talkative, — he who had never spoken to a woman who had not passed her sixtieth year, — his eyes devoured them; he was eager to hear every word that they were saying.

" Ah, my dear, what a pretty coiffure you have! My stingy old husband has been to Snizily, and he brought me back some embroidered trousers. I am wrong to call him stingy, for he is not so with me; he refuses me nothing that I ask of him. It is true that he is very exacting, and that, for my part, I do just as he wishes."

" Do you know, Fatima," said another, " that my old ape of a husband has taken a second wife at Baku? I began to weep and reproach him. Guess what he answered me? ' Can I go without rice?' Oh! I shall have my revenge. He takes a second wife, the old rascal, and is in no condition to observe Saturday with me. Not he, my dear, no. It is incredible, is it not? But that is the way. By the by, do you know that a ukase has been issued in Russia ordering the women to wear trousers? I have myself seen ladies in Derbend with white trousers all embroidered and open-worked. — It was high time! They were scandalous to behold when the wind blew."

" Oh! how good that soap is you gave me, my dear Sheker!" said a third; " and how grateful I am to you for it! Fancy, since using that, my skin has become like satin."

" Ah, well, yes, she is dead," a fourth was saying; " he killed her, so much the worse for her. When she fell in love with some one else, she ought to have known how to keep it to herself. As soon as her husband left the house, she went visiting, with a lantern, too. Faith! he killed her in short order."

"Ah, my dear," said a fifth, "how my children worry me! I never saw children grow so fast! To look at them, one would think I was an old woman; and they have sore heads, besides. You understand; I have never had a pimple myself; it comes from their father."

"Ah! your little children may trouble you with their heads, but mine trouble me with their hearts. Mégely torments me beyond measure; he will give me no peace until I buy him a wife."

"Ah well, buy one for the boy; he is tall and old enough to have a wife. I saw him pass just yesterday."

"You are a silly one, you are! You talk as if a wife called for two kopecks. A wife costs something. Where shall I get the money, pray?"

"Ah!" cried a sixth, "what a shame! and you say, my dear, that she is with an Armenian? Are there no more Mussulmans or Russians, then?"

"How kind my husband is! if you but knew," said a seventh; "and he is so handsome! he might be taken for the prophet himself, and although large — "

Iskander listened so intently that he almost forgot why he was there. But the cries, "They are beginning! they are beginning!" put an end to all chattering.

Each turned to the stage and gave her attention to the play. Yazíd, in red caftan and green turban, was seated on his throne. Below him, at his left, standing on the fourth step of his throne, was the European ambassador, represented by Yussef in a fantastic costume, whose conspicuous features consisted of a three-cornered hat surmounted by an immense plume, an enormous sword, and spurs six inches long.

Yazíd's suite, composed of white-turbaned super-numeraries, formed a semi-circle about his throne.

But not Yazíd's self upon his throne, not the magnificent white-turbaned suite, produced an effect to be compared with that of Yussef, with a hat that would not keep its balance on his shaven pate, a sword he knew not where to put, and spurs that tore the trousers of the noblest and gravest lords of Yazíd's court.

But what especially excited great hilarity among the men, and the liveliest discussion among the women, was that gigantic nose and that colossal plume.

" Oh, look, sister," said a little girl of rank, " look at that creature beside Yazíd!  What kind of beast does he represent ? "

" That is a lion, you silly child," responded the sister.  " Did you not know that the abominable tyrant, Yazíd, that brute among caliphs, always had a lion near him ?  If any one incurred his displeasure, he was thrown to the lion, who ate him up.  Come, listen, there is Yazíd saying to Hussein, ' Adopt my religion or you shall die ! '  Hussein sneezes, which signifies, ' I will not. ' "

" That 's not a lion," pursued the insistent little one; " lions have n't beaks; it 's a bird."

" A bird with a tail on his head !  Have you ever seen birds with tails on their heads ? "

" Yes; it 's a top-knot."

" It 's a mane."

" The child is right," said a third, entering upon the discussion.  " Can you not see that it is a parrot ?  This parrot was interpreting secretary at Yazíd's court.  Do you not see how the caliph caresses him ? "

" Then why does he shout like the devil ? "

" Oh, do keep still, now, parrots of nieces that you

are!" said a good Tartar dame weighing one hundred and fifty kilogrammes, and occupying the space of four ordinary people, with whom listening for herself was like listening for a whole society.

The dispute became general at this juncture. Some continued to maintain that it was a lion, others contended that it was a bird; but Yussef ought to have felt highly flattered that the general opinion held him to be some sort of an animal.

He, little suspecting the flutter which he heard to be occasioned by his own nose and feathers, was discoursing meanwhile with the tyrant.

"My king," he was saying, "the ruler of France, having heard of your conquests, sends me to offer you his friendship."

Yazíd answered: "Let your king cease to eat pork, let him forbid his allies to eat it, and let him order them to become Mussulmans."

"But if his friends refuse?" replied the ambassador.

"Then let him introduce my system."

"Let us see your system," demanded the ambassador.

"Bring me my system," said Yazíd.

An executioner entered, naked sword in hand.

Yussef shook his head.

"What do you mean by that?" demanded Yazíd.

"I mean, great prince, that your system would not succeed in Europe."

"Why not?"

"Because it would be impossible to cut off a European's head as you would an Arab's."

"Impossible?" said Yazíd. "You shall see whether it is impossible."

And, turning to his guards and the executioner, he commanded. —

" Take the European ambassador and cut off his head, that he may see that my system is adapted to every country."

Guards and executioner advanced towards Yussef; but he had so recently taken part in a similar drama with Mullah Nour, that fact and fancy became confused in mind and sight; when he saw the guards about to lay hands on him, he wanted to run away; when he saw the executioner raise his sword, he emitted piercing shrieks.   He was arrested when about to leap from the stage into the street, and brought back amid the frantic applause of the multitude, who had never seen terror simulated with such fidelity.

He was still heard calling Iskander to his rescue long after he had gone behind the scenes.

But Iskander had quite another affair on hand.

Iskander had at last got next to Kassime.   He could scarcely breathe for joy; his heart was burning; he felt the warmth of Kassime's cheeks; he inhaled the perfume of her breath.

What could you expect?   He was in love; he was twenty years old; he loved for the first time.

But he could contain himself no longer when, in shifting her position to be more at her ease, Kassime leaned her hand on his knee.

" Kassime," he whispered in her ear, " I must speak with you."

And he gently pressed her hand.

The young girl's heart and head were full of Iskander; she was hoping to see him at this fête, at which all Derbend was present.   She had not come for Yazíd's sake; no caliph's executioner was occupying her mind.

Her eyes had searched for Iskander on all sides, but he was nowhere to be seen.

Imagine, then, her amazement, fancy her joy when she heard in her ear that well-known, that beloved voice !

She had not the strength to resist.

Iskander rose; she followed him.   He led her to the darkest corner of the roof.

Those around were so occupied with Yazíd that there was nothing to fear.

Yet Iskander understood that he had no time to lose.

"Kassime," said he, "do you know how I love you? do you know how I worship you?   You see what I have risked for the sake of seeing you for one moment, for the sake of saying a few words to you.   Then consider what I am capable of doing if you say, ' Iskander, I love you not.'   Yes, or no, Kassime? yes, or no?"

Iskander's eyes flashed lightnings through his veil; his left hand pressed Kassime's waist, his right rested on his pistol.   The poor child trembled as she looked about her.

"Iskander," said she, "I ask of you but two things, — do not kill me, do not disgrace me!   I would gladly clasp you in my arms as closely as your sword belt; but you know my uncle."

Then, urged on in spite of herself, after a moment's hesitation, she added, —

"Iskander, I love you!"

And, like steel to the magnet, her lips were drawn to those of the young man.

"And now," said she, "let me go."

"So be it; but on one condition, my darling, — that we meet here to-morrow night."

Kassime answered nothing; but the word *to-morrow* was so clearly revealed in the look which she gave her friend at parting, that Iskander took the rendezvous for granted.

I cannot tell you how Kassime passed the night; but Iskander's sleep was very sweet.

There are some sins after which we sleep better than after the best of good works.

## XII.

### ACCUSED AND ACQUITTED.

Two days after the fête, there was a large meeting in the fortress of Narin Kale, near the commandant's house.

Armed noukars held their masters' horses by the bridle; there were people in the courts, about the fountain, on the stairs; the salon was full of visitors, and these visitors were the leading people of the town. At the entrance door the commandant's interpreter was eagerly rehearsing something extraordinary, no doubt, for he was listened to and questioned. Elsewhere, they spoke in low tones. The old men shrugged their shoulders; in short, it was easy to see that something strange and out of the common was taking place, or had already taken place.

"Yes," said the interpreter, "this is exactly how the thing was done. The brigands made a hole in the wall and entered the room of Soliman Beg. He awoke, but only when one of the robbers was in the act of taking down the arms that hung above his head. Soliman then drew a pistol from under his pillow and fired, but the ball hit no one. Meanwhile, two or three other bandits were binding his wife in a neighboring room. Hearing the shot, they rushed out and came to the aid of the two who were in Soliman's room. The darkness interfered with the effectiveness of his shots, yet Soliman wounded two or three of the bandits: however, he himself fell dead under four or five dagger-thrusts. The shooting, and the cries of Soliman and his wife, awoke the neighbors; but while they were dressing, lighting their lanterns, and rushing to Soliman's house, the robbers had broken into his coffers and emptied them, and they were gone without having been seen, and, consequently, without a single one's having been identified."

"So not one of the knaves has been arrested?" demanded a new-comer.

"No; and yet it is believed that an accomplice is caught."

"An accomplice?"

"Yes; he had been stationed as a watch; he had a rope around him, for the purpose no doubt of aiding his comrades in scaling the wall. He carried a pistol and a dagger in his belt; but it must be admitted that, as a beg, he had a right to carry arms."

"What! a beg? But it is impossible that a beg should be an accomplice of thieves!" cried several voices at once.

"And why is it impossible?" replied a mirza, casting around him the scoffing glance so much affected by Tartar youths.

"Yes; but this one is really a beg belonging to one of the best families in Derbend, and you will indeed be astonished when I tell you his name. It is Iskander Ben Kalfasi Ogli. Wait, at this very moment the commandant is reading the report of the chief of police, and you will presently see Iskander; an order has been given to bring him here."

In fact, the news astonished everybody. Iskander was greatly pitied. How could a young man whose conduct was so irreproachable, who had been chosen to bring the snow from Schach Dagh, be the accomplice of such bandits ?

The commandant's entrance put a stop to all discussion, and a profound silence was established. He was one of those men who thoroughly understand the Asiatic character. He was discriminately affable, the better to make his affability appreciated, severe without the rudeness that envenoms justice, even when she is just.

He entered the salon in full uniform.

All the by-standers saluted him, placing their hands over their hearts and letting them fall to the knee.

The commandant bowed to all, and spoke briefly on current matters. Some he gently chided for inefficient service; others he thanked for having performed their duties conscientiously; he pressed the hands of some of the Derbend freeholders, — there are freeholders everywhere, — and invited two of them to dine with him the next day.

Then, addressing himself to all, he said, —

" Gentlemen begs, I suppose you all know what took place last night. I have every reason to think it an enterprise of our friends the mountaineers, and not the deed of residents of Derbend. I entreat you all to do your utmost to capture the thieves and bring them before me. Well," he added, turning to the mirza, " has the mullah questioned Iskander ? In that case, what has the beg to say ? "

" Iskander naturally replies that he is as innocent as a new-born babe of this whole affair. He says that he carried the rope to get outside of the city for a walk, and climb back again whenever he pleased, because, he asserts, the air of the city is stifling. As to his arms, he gave no other explanation than this: ' As a beg, I have a right to carry them.' "

9

" A singular walk, that," said the commandant, " with a rope around the loins! and yet I must say the whole of Iskander's past conduct is a protest against the crime of which he is accused. I wish to see and question him myself; bring him in."

Iskander Beg entered, his papak on his head, according to the Asiatic custom; he bowed respectfully to the commandant, haughtily to the people, and waited in the place assigned to him.

The commandant regarded him coldly. At the thought of being an object of suspicion, the young beg could not help blushing; but his eye was steady and clear.

" I little suspected, Iskander," said the commandant, " that I should ever see you brought before me as a criminal."

" It is not crime, but fate, that brings me here," replied Iskander.

" Do you know the consequences of the crime of which you are accused ? "

" Only here have I learned of my supposed crime. I acknowledge my imprudence; appearances are against me, I am aware; but guilty? God knows I am not! "

" Unfortunately, Iskander," returned the commandant, " men must be governed by appearances, and until your innocence is proved, you are in the hands of justice. However, if there is any one here who will answer for you, I will consent to your going at liberty."

Iskander cast a questioning glance around; but no one offered to become his surety.

" What! " said the commandant, " not one ? "

" At your pleasure, commandant," replied the bystanders, bowing.

" Well, I will answer for him myself, and be his bondsman," said Hadji Yussef, coming forward.

The commandant smiled; the lookers-on laughed aloud; but the commandant frowned, and the faces grew long.

" Truly, I am astonished, gentlemen," said the commandant, " that you, who so readily give bail for the greatest rascals to be found in our city, for wretches who have twenty times fled to the mountains after you have gone on their bonds, should hesitate to do as much for a young man whom, eight days ago, you recognized as the purest and most upright among you. His good reputation will not save him from chastisement; on the contrary, if he is guilty, he shall be severely punished. But until he is convicted, he is your compeer, and his exemplary life should be respected. Go home, Iskander; if you had not found security, I should have served you myself."

The commandant saluted the assembly and set off for the mosque.

The young beg went home, his eyes dimmed with tears of gratitude.

The morning sun gilded the porch of the mosque of Derbend. The old men were warming themselves in its vivifying rays as they talked of bygone days; two or three beggars had halted at the entrance of the court.

A few steps farther on, a wayfarer was sleeping under his bourka; not far from the traveller sat Mullah Sédek on his rug.

The holy man was ready to leave Derbend the next morning, and was reckoning up from memory all the small profits by which his journey had enriched him. While mentally recalling the trifling items, he was eating a sort of pastry which he dipped into a dish of garlic and milk. From time to time he plunged his reed pen into a wooden ink-bottle, and wrote a few words on a little scrap of paper that he had beside him. It was curious to note with what appetite the holy man ate his breakfast, and with what pleasure he footed up his accounts.

He was so deeply engrossed in this twofold enjoyment that he did not see a poor Lesghian before him begging for alms. The wretch was asking for a kopeck in such pitiful accents that it was truly a crime to deny him.

Mullah Sédek finally heard the sort of litany that the poor devil was chanting; he raised his eyes, but almost as quickly lowered them again to his accounts.

" For three days I have had nothing to eat, master," the Lesghian was saying, as he held out his hand.

"Ten, twenty-five, fifty, one hundred," counted Mullah Sédek.

" A kopeck will save my life and open the gates of Paradise to you."

"One hundred, five hundred, one thousand," continued Mullah Sédek.

" You are a mullah," persisted the Lesghian; " recall what the Koran says: ' The first duty of a Mussulman is charity.' "

Mullah Sédek lost his patience.

"Go to the devil!" he angrily exclaimed. "Was it for wretches like you that Allah invented charity? You have sticks in the town and herbs in the fields. When you are strong enough, you rob; otherwise, you ask alms, and they are no sooner given than you laugh at the fool that gave. You will get nothing from me; I am a poor traveller, too, and all that I had has been taken away by your brigand of a Mullah Nour."

The wayfarer lying under his bourka, who had not said a word until then, quietly raised himself, and stroking his beard with his hand, he politely demanded of Mullah Sédek, —

"Has Mullah Nour been so cruel as to leave you absolutely without money, — a holy man like you? Yet I have heard it said that Mullah Nour is a conscientious man, and that he rarely takes more than two roubles from one traveller."

"Two roubles! that rapacious Mullah Nour! Trust yourself in his hands and you will be very lucky if he does not pick out your two eyes. Would that he might be struck down by the destroying angel, and boil throughout all eternity in the gold that he took from me, even if I had to melt the gold myself. Did he not take even my aba of camel's-hair?"

"That is true," said the old men. "Mullah Sédek came to us without an aba and with only his mantle; we have done our best to reclothe him. Curses on this Mullah Nour!"

The wayfarer with the bourka arose smiling, and drawing a piece of gold from his pocket he held it out to the Lesghian, saying, —

"Curse Mullah Nour as these honest men have just done, and this *tchervoniès* is yours."

The Lesghian at first extended his hand; but almost instantly withdrew it, shaking his head, and replied, —

"No, Mullah Nour has helped my brother in misfortune, — he gave him a hundred roubles; on ten occasions he has aided my compatriots. I do not know his

face, but I know his heart. Keep your gold, I will
not curse Mullah Nour. I sell neither my benedictions
nor my maledictions."

The wayfarer regarded the beggar with astonishment,
and Mullah Sédek with scorn.

Then, drawing out four other gold pieces, which he
added to the first, he gave them all five to the poor
Lesghian.

Thereupon, resting one hand on Mullah Sédek's
shoulder, and pointing with the other above his head,
he said, —

"In heaven there is a God of truth, and on earth are
some good men."

After which, picking up his bourka, he threw it over
his shoulder, mounted his horse, which had been tied
to the mosque wall, and slowly descended to the
bazaar.

Then, having crossed the bazaar, always at a walk,
he entered the street in which was to be found the house
of the chief of police.

This official was at his door, surrounded by several
persons to whom he was doling out justice; he was
already old, but so black did he keep his beard that
he was himself deluded as to his age, and fancied that
he was at least ten years younger than he was. His
tchourka was trimmed with lace, no more nor less than
that of a man of fashion, and, as a much livelier
reminder of his youth, he still had four wives and three
mistresses, and drank several bottles of wine every
evening. In short, had he not worn spectacles, had he
not been as wrinkled as an old apple, had he not had a
paunch like a pumpkin, one might have believed, after
what he himself had said, in the youth of this most
worthy man.

That day his Excellency was in a bad humor; he was in a rage with everybody, and quarrelled even with the passers-by.

It was in this state of mind that he saw a traveller dismount from his horse and approach him.

"*Salaam Aleikoum*, Mouzaram Beg!" was the way-farer's greeting.

The chief of police shook as if he had been stung by a scorpion, and laid his hand on his pistol.

But the traveller bent down to his ear and said, —

"Mouzaram Beg, if I were to give you a bit of advice, it would be that you do not meddle with old friends. I have come, too, for your own good; I can do you a service, only, let us go within. I can tell you something for which all Derbend will thank me. But if you make a doubtful sign, you know my pistol carries a ball, and that that ball goes, too, just where I wish it to go, as surely as if, instead of placing it with the eye, I were to place it with my finger. At the first move, then, I fire. I appear to be alone, but do not trust to that. A dozen of my brave men keep me in sight, and at my first summons they will be here. Come, lead the way, Mouzaram Beg."

The chief of police made no protest and went in first.

What took place then? The interview was without witnesses; no one can tell.

We know only that a quarter of an hour after entering, the unknown came out, calmly mounted his horse, threw a silver rouble to the noukar who had held the bridle, and left the city.

But two days later it was told how the celebrated brigand Mullah Nour had had the audacity to enter the city; how, thanks to his active surveillance, the chief of police had been warned of his presence, and had sent after him a dozen noukars, to whom Mullah Nour was glad to show his horse's heels.

Ill-bred people said much worse; but one never has to believe what ill-bred people say.

During this time poor Iskander was moping within the four walls of his house. He had but to say one word to establish his innocence; but he would a hundred times have preferred to die rather than dishonor Kassime.

To await trial is purgatory for every native of Asia. An Asiatic can better sustain an undeserved punishment than a merited trial if the latter is delayed.

" Ah! " he cried in his impatience, " eternal chains, the snows of Siberia, everything rather than the suspicion of the Russians, who force me to love them, and the mockery of my compatriots, whom I detest. I am ready to die by the sword, but to die by the rope is to die twice. "

And, bound by his parole, he began to roar and rage like a caged tiger, to rend the sleeves of his tchourka and weep like a child.

In the evening, at an hour when all the streets in the city were empty, when the houses were enlivened by the sound of voices and the flashing of lights, when the married Mussulman was enjoying repose of soul beside his wife, — even beside the four wives allotted him by the prophet, — and when, on the other hand, the celibate was moping at his hearth, Iskander, sitting by his own with his head thrust between his two hands, heard one of his window-panes crash under a blow from some object, and that object fell into his room.

It was a pebble, to which was attached a small note.

He unfolded it. and read. —

"Mullah Nour to Iskander, greeting! Better to be a captive and innocent, than a free man and guilty, believe me.

"I know all; I will declare everything in order to prove your innocence.

"The rest lies with Allah!

"Patience and hope; your deliverance shall not be long in coming."

The next morning, Iskander was summoned before the commandant; but he had not had time to arrive before every one was already congratulating him upon the happy turn in his affairs.

The robbers were captured; they had got together to divide the booty at Baktiara, where they had been surrounded and made prisoners.

Two were Lesghians, two were men of that city.

In the house of one of the latter was a double wall in which the plunder had been secreted.

Iskander Beg was quite innocent.

Then Iskander, deeply touched by the kindly regard bestowed on him by the commandant, in turn sought a private interview. He confessed all, — his love for Kassime, Festahli's broken promise.

The commandant listened, half smiling, half sad.

"Iskander," said he, "you see yourself into what your imprudence has led you. Festahli did wrong, doubtless; but one is not avenged of a wrong by doing wrong. Thieves of gold are not the only thieves; an upright man does nothing underhandedly. Secrecy and night are the cloaks of ravishers and brigands. Your future happiness occupies your heart; I shall do what I can to make it expand from your heart into your life. Adieu, Iskander. In the name of those who love you, remain what you are, and what you nearly ceased to be, — an honest man!"

And he pressed his hand affectionately, again wishing him happiness.

Iskander was proclaimed innocent, Iskander was free; his enjoyment of the twofold happiness lasted but a moment.    It was such grief for the young man to believe that he must renounce his Kassime.

The kiss that he had snatched from her lips thrilled him yet to the depths of his heart.   He recalled minutely every detail of his last meeting with his beloved; his soul seemed ready to fly at the thought of that sweet voice whose echo it had become.

" No," said he, " Mullah Nour has written nonsense, and as for what the commandant told me, it is easily seen that he is not in love.    I am ready to purchase Kassime even with a crime, and I am sure that in spite of the crime I should be happy with her, — happy, even if I should be forced to carry her to the mountain, with her consent or without it.    I will take her away, if only for an hour; I will steep my heart in heavenly delights."

Poor Kassime was sorrowful also.    In her solitude she was learning with tears to count the hours of separation.

" I fastened a rose on my breast," sighed she, " and it whispered, ' I am the Spring;' a nightingale sang me his song of love, and I called it joy; Iskander looked into my eyes and gave me a kiss, and with that kiss I knew love.    But where art thou, lovely rose? where art thou, sweet nightingale? where art thou, Iskander? They are gone where my happiness has flown."

# XIII.

## THE MILLER.

KNOW you the Tengua?

It is sometimes a brooklet, sometimes a torrent, some-times a stream, and at times a river.

For a quarter of a verst it runs cramped within a narrow gorge, into which it plunges with abhorrence, and through which it madly courses.

The storms of many centuries have not washed the blackened traces of lightning from the walls of the gorge where the Tengua thunders.

Entire masses of rock, precipitated from the mountain's height to the bottom of the gorge, form the bed over which it leaps and foams with maddening uproar.

The neighborhood of this chasm is wild and gloomy; its entrance is formidable.

The right bank of the torrent casts the shadow of its rocks far over the valley.

The left bank lowers into the water a narrow path which first traverses a little wood.

Ill luck to the horseman who, without guide, engages in a struggle with this liquid hell, especially at seasons of thaw or melting snow.

Ill luck to him if he encounter brigands in this pass, which seems expressly planned for an ambuscade. De fence and flight are impossible here.

At this spot Mullah Nour, the bandit from the book of whose life we are taking a page, — this very Mullah

Nour with a dozen of his fellows stopped three regiments which were returning with the enormous spoils of General Pankratief's expedition.

When they were just on the point of descending into the river, he appeared before them mounted and completely armed, threw his bourka on the ground and said, —

"I salute you, comrades! Allah has granted you victory and spoils. Honor be to you! but it would only be like the good Christians you are to let me share your happiness. I exact nothing, — I entreat; be generous, and let each give me what he will. Think now, brothers, you are returning rich, carrying presents to your relatives. As for me, I am poor, I have no home; and for an hour's repose under others' roofs, I pay a handful of gold. Yet, know you, brothers, men have, like cowards, stripped me of everything. Happily, Allah has preserved my courage; more than that, he has given me these gloomy ravines and these naked rocks which you yourselves scorn. Of these rocks and ravines I am king, and no one shall pass through my territories without my permission. You are in great numbers, you are brave; but if you mean to pass by force, it will cost you much blood, and of time much more, for you will cross only when I and my brave men have fallen. Every stone will fight for me, and as for myself, I will shed here the last drop of my blood; I will burn here my last grain of powder. Choose; you have much to lose, and I nothing. Men call me Nour, *The Light*, but my life, I swear, is gloomier than the darkness."

A murmur rose from the ranks of the troopers; some frowned, others were wrathful.

"Let us trample Mullah Nour under our horses'

feet," said they, "and go on. You see how many we are, how many you are. On! let us charge the bandits!"

But no one ventured first into the roaring stream, whose ford was covered by the guns of a dozen brigands.

Rashness made way for reflection, and the three regiments yielded to Mullah Nour's demands.

"We shall give you what we like, and nothing more."

And so saying, each cavalier threw a little money down on the bandit's bourka.

"But understand that, by force, you could not have taken a nail from our horses' shoes."

And they passed one by one in single file before Mullah Nour.

Mullah Nour smilingly bowed to them.

"Allah!" said he, after this adventure which had brought him three or four thousand roubles, "it is no feat to shear the wool from the sheep of Daghestan, when I have shaved the hair from the wolves of the Karabach. I do not know why these people of Daghestan should complain about their crops; I take no pains to sow, plough, or cultivate; I stand on the highway and pray, and my prayer brings me an ample harvest. Only know how to set about it, and you can extract an abassi, not from every carriage, but from every gun-barrel."

But early in the summer of the year in which the events that we are relating took place, no one had seen Mullah Nour, no one had heard Mullah Nour spoken of as on the banks of the Tengua. Where was he, then?

In the government of Shekin perhaps; perhaps in Persia, where he might indeed have been forced to take refuge; and perhaps he was dead.

Nobody knew anything about him, — not even Mullah Sédek, who pretended to have been robbed by him on his way from Persia to Derbend.

He had left Kouban early in the morning, this worthy, this respectable Mullah Sédek, and, toward noon, he had reached the spot where the Tengua, freed from the confines of the gorge, goes on its way. Insatiate as the desert sand, he was unwilling to take a guide, whose trouble he must have paid for by a few paltry pieces of the coin that he had gathered by the bushel at Derbend.

The June sun was terribly warm, and our wayfaring mullah was in the act of transferring his gun from the right shoulder to the left.

When he caught sight of a little wood in the distance, he was delighted; but when he saw the river close at hand, he was in despair.

" May the devil take me! " murmured he; " had I known what this river was like, I would not have attempted to cross it without a guide, although its bed were silver and gold instead of rocks. In fact, I was crazy not to have hired one."

And he gazed about him in terror; the spot was deserted and solitary.

However, after careful search, he discovered, tied to a tree in the wood, a horse all saddled and bridled; and under this same tree was a simple Tartar, armed only with his kandjiar, a weapon that no Tartar ever goes without.

Mullah Sédek approached step by step and looked attentively.

The flour whitening the Tartar's coat and beard indicated that he was a miller. The miller was eating his breakfast.

Our holy man, who had felt his heart beat for an instant, became reassured.

"Hi! friend!" cried he to the unknown, "it seems to me that you belong hereabouts, do you not?"

"To be sure I belong here," replied the miller with his mouth full.

"In that case, you ought to know all the fords of this river?"

"Oh! I certainly think I ought to know the fords of the Tengua; she runs only with my permission. Such as you see her, this river is my servant."

"You will do me a great service, my good man, and Allah will bless you, if you will conduct me to the other side of the gorge."

"Wait until night," tranquilly returned the miller. "Between now and night the river will fall, my horse will be rested, and I, too, shall be refreshed. It will not take us more than a quarter of an hour then to ford the torrent; but just now it is dangerous."

"In the name of Allah! In the names of Ali and Hussein! In the name of my prayers! I am a mullah; lead me across without delay, now, instantly!"

"Oh!" said the miller, "neither prayers nor blessings will bring that to pass. Never, at such high water, will I try to ford the Tengua!"

"Have some feeling, my friend; Allah will reward you, you may be sure, if you do anything for a mullah."

"Mullah as much as you like, but I would not risk getting drowned to guide the prophet himself."

"Do not despise me; I am not so poor as you think, perhaps, and if you render me this service, it shall not be for nothing."

The miller smiled.

"Well, let us see, what would you give me?" he said, scratching his beard.

"I will give you two abassis; I hope that is reasonable."

"Good! two abassis? With two abassis I should not even have the means of getting my horse shod. No, I will not take you across for two roubles even; because a new head is not to be bought with two roubles, and a man would plainly be risking his head in that frightful ford."

They bargained a long time; at last Mullah Sédek ended by promising the sum exacted by the miller.

On giving up his horse's bridle to the guide, Mullah Sédek surrendered at discretion and trusted himself entirely to the other's experience. The holy man nearly died of fright when he began to ford the river and penetrated the entrance of the gorge. But when, through the opposite gap, he again caught sight of the valley covered with grass, with sunlight and flowers, his courage revived, and supposing there was nothing more to fear, he addressed his guide, —

"Come, will you get on a little faster, you rascal?"

But our brave mullah had found his courage a little too soon. The last part of the ford was the deepest and most dangerous.

The guide halted just at that part, and turning his horse, he said, —

"Well, Sédek, ten steps more and you are on the bank. Now let us settle our accounts. You know that I have well earned your gold-piece, eh?"

"A gold-piece! Have you no conscience, friend? No, you are joking, surely. I might as well have built me a silver bridge to cross on. Go on, now, good fellow, and on the other side I will give you two abassis and you can be off."

" Good! we shall come to better terms, I fancy."

" Undoubtedly, undoubtedly. Necessity — you hold a knife to my throat, and I must certainly cross over. Where do you expect a poor traveller to get so much money? Alas! I have already been robbed. Come, come, take me to the other side, brother; and once there, you can go about your business, and I will go about mine."

" Not so," said the miller, shaking his head; " I told you, and I repeat that I will not leave this spot without having settled my account with you, and our account does not date from to-day. You have no conscience, Mullah Sédek, but you doubtless have a memory. To excite sympathy and obtain money at Derbend, you invented the story that Mullah Nour had stopped you, stripped you, and taken everything. Tell me, where did that happen?"

" I have never said such a thing!" cried Mullah Sédek; " may Allah condemn me if I said that!"

" Recall the court of the mosque, Sédek; remember what you said to the Lesghian, what you told the wayfarer who slept on his bourka. And now look me in the face, as I am looking at you, and perhaps we shall recognize each other."

Mullah Sédek scanned the face of his guide; under the flour which covered it he was at first unrecognizable, but the flour had disappeared; gradually the whitened beard had become black; under the frowning brows glittered two black eyes. However, seeing that he had no weapon but his kandjiar, Mullah Sédek seized his gun; but before he could cock it, the kandjiar's point was at his breast.

"If you twitch so much as a hair of your moustache," said the counterfeit miller, "I warn you that, like Jonah, you shall go to preach to the fishes against drinking either wine or brandy. Come, now, away with your gun, away with your sword! Your business is to cheat people in the shops and in the pulpit; to lie in the morning, to lie in the evening, to lie at all times; but fighting is the business of brave men, — not yours, therefore. Do not move, I say, you son of a dog! In this place, there is no need for me to waste even one charge of powder on you, and that is why I carry no fire-arms; I have only to drop your horse's bridle, and in five minutes you are a corpse."

At these words Mullah Sédek turned as white as wax. He clutched his horse's mane, conscious that he was growing dizzy, and about to slip from his saddle. But, without for an instant losing sight of the wicked kandjiar that glittered against his breast like a flashing light, he cried, —

"Mercy! I am a mullah!"

"I am myself a mullah," responded the guide, "and even more than a mullah, — I am Mullah Nour."

Mullah Sédek gave a shriek and cowered to his horse's mane, clasping both hands about his own neck, as if he already felt the steel's sharp edge upon its nape.

Mullah Nour began to laugh at Sédek's terror; then raising him up at last, he said, —

"Your story to the people of Derbend maligned me; you made everybody believe that I had robbed you of your last kopeck, of your last shirt even, — I, who give the poor man the bit of bread that he begs in vain at the rich man's door, — I who never take more than one piece of gold from the merchants themselves, and that not for myself, but for my comrades, — comrades who would kill and plunder without shame and without remorse, did I not restrain them. And more than that, — you are the robber, for you meant to rob your guide by refusing him what you had promised; lastly, you are an assassin, for when I demanded what was legitimately my due you would have assassinated me."

" Have pity on me, pardon me, good Mullah Nour!" said Sédek.

" Have you ever pitied the lot of the poor man whom you saw dying of hunger? Would you have felt any remorse if you had killed me? No; for you are a miserable wretch. You coin every letter of the Koran into money, and in your own interests and for your own profit you sow dissension in families. I recognized you; I knew what sort of a man you were, and I did not touch you when you passed along here on your way to Derbend. You did not see me; you did not meet me; you did not know me; yet you insulted me. Well, now you will not be lying when you say that I have robbed you. Mullah Sédek, give me your money!"

Mullah Sédek sent up shriek after shriek, he shed great tears; but he was entrapped, he had to submit. One after another, he cast his poor roubles into the sack held out to him by Mullah Nour, squeezing each coin before letting it go, as if a coating of silver might cling to his hands.

Finally, he reached the last piece.

" That is all," said he.

" You would swear to a lie on the edge of the grave!" cried Mullah Nour. " Look here, Sédek, unless you wish to become more intimately acquainted with my poniard, count better. You still have money; you have gold in the inside pocket of your tchouska. I know how much, and I can tell you, — fifteen hundred roubles. Is n't that it ? "

Great was the lamentation of Sédek, but he was forced to yield up his very last piece of gold.

Mullah Nour had spoken the truth, he knew the amount.

Mullah Nour then conducted Sédek to the much desired bank, and made him there dismount from his horse.

Mullah Sédek believed himself at quits with the bandit, but he was deceived.

" Now, that is not all," said the latter; " you have hindered the marriage of Iskander Beg, and you must mend what you have marred.   You have a bottle of ink in your girdle; write to Hadji Festahli that you have received on the way a letter from your brother, in which he tells you that his son does not wish to marry, and has gone on a pilgrimage to Mecca; or say that he is dead, if you like.   The deuce! you ought not to be put to it for a lie!   Only, arrange it so that Iskander can wed his promised bride.   Otherwise, I shall see to marrying you to the houris, Mullah Sédek! "

" Never! " cried Mullah Sédek, " never!   No, no, no, I will not do it!   You have taken all I had; be content with what you have robbed me of."

" Ah! is it so ? " said Mullah Nour.

He clapped his hands three times, and, at the third, a dozen bandits appeared, as if they had issued from the rocks.

" The worthy Mullah Sédek wishes to write," said Mullah Nour; " second him, my friends, in the laudable intention."

In a twinkling, Mullah Sédek, if such was indeed his desire, had nothing left to wish for.   One bandit

detached his ink-bottle, another dipped his pen in the
ink, a third handed him paper, and last of all, a fourth,
bracing his hands against his knees, and lowering his
shoulders, offered his back for a desk.

Three times Mullah Sédek began to write, but,
whether from errors or unwillingness, three times he
broke off.

"Well?" demanded Mullah Nour, his voice but the
more threatening for appearing to be perfectly calm.

"The ink is bad, and my head is so bothered that I
can think of no words."

"Then write with your blood and think with your
papak," said Mullah Nour, with an emphasizing flash
of the terrible kandjiar; "but write very quickly! If
not, I will put such a point between your two eyebrows
that the devil alone can tell which letter of the alphabet
you resemble."

Mullah Sédek saw that his hesitation had gone its
length, and he finally made up his mind to write.

"Set your seal now," said Mullah Nour, when the
letter was finished.

Mullah Sédek obeyed.

"There! now give it to me," demanded Mullah Nour;
"I will see to posting it."

He took the letter, read it, assured himself that it
was what he desired, thrust it into his pocket, and then,
tossing to Mullah Sédek all that had been taken from
him, he said, —

"There is your gold and silver, Sédek; take it back,
not a kopeck is missing. And now which of us two is
miser or thief? Answer. However, it is not a gift,
but a payment. You have blackened my name at
Derbend, you must regild it at Schumaka, and that in
open mosque. Go, then, and know that if you do not

carry out my orders, my ball will find you, however well hidden you may be. I have convinced you that I know everything; I will prove to you that I can do everything."

Mullah Sédek pledged himself to all that the bandit exacted, took possession of his money very joyfully, restored it to his pockets, after first assuring himself that his pockets contained no holes, and, remounting his horse, he set off at full gallop.

Two days later, Mullah Sédek scandalized the people of Schumaka by a discourse in which he eulogized Mullah Nour, comparing him to a lion that bore the heart of a dove in his breast.

## XIV.

### CONCLUSION.

PROBABLY the letter written to Festahli by his friend, Mullah Sédek, left the former not a ray of hope for the union on which he had counted; for, one evening after the letter had reached his address, music and songs were heard in the streets of Derbend.

Kassime was being escorted to the home of her betrothed husband, Iskander.

All Derbend followed her; shouts and acclamations rent the air on every side, and from every house-top innumerable guns discharged their fires, like brilliant rockets.

The whole town seemed ablaze, rejoicing in Iskander's happiness.

Iskander Beg, on hearing the noise and music, had twenty times drawn near to his door, and every time custom forbade his opening it.

Finally, at the twenty-first time, when the procession was almost at his threshold, as he half-opened his door and shyly put out his head, a horseman extended his hand, saying, —

"Iskander, may Allah grant you all the happiness that I wish you!"

And the same instant he wheeled his horse away, that he might not be caught in the midst of the crowd.

But, just as the horse turned, he found himself face to face with Yussef, who, naturally, was the best man at Iskander's wedding.

Yussef Beg recognized the horseman, and could not restrain an exclamation of terror.

"Mullah Nour!" he cried.

That name, as one can well understand, threw the fête into great confusion.

The cry "Mullah Nour! Mullah Nour!" re-echoed on all sides.

"This way! that way! catch him! hold him fast!" howled the ten thousand voices together.

But Mullah Nour shot away like a flash of lightning.

All the young men who were on horseback in the bride's train dashed off in pursuit of the bandit.

Mullah Nour flew through the streets of Derbend, and all they saw of him in the dark was the shower of sparks from his horse's hoofs.

But as the city gates were closed Mullah Nour could not get out.

By the glare of shots fired at him along his course, they saw that he was headed toward the sea.

He would there find himself caught between the ramparts and the water.

One instant the bandit paused; the sea was high. They saw the leaping waves and tossing foam; they heard their roar.

"He is caught! he is ours! Death to Mullah Nour!" shouted his pursuers.

But Mullah Nour's whip whistled like the wind, flashed like the lightning, and from the rock where he had an instant paused, at one leap his horse plunged into the sea.

His pursuers drew rein as the waters of the Caspian Sea washed their horses' flanks.

They strained their eyes, screening them with their hands, in an effort to pierce the gloom.

" He is lost! drowned! dead! " they shouted at last.

A formidable peal of laughter answered their shouts, and a hurrah sent up from a dozen throats was heard in the direction of a little island uprising about a quarter of a verst from Derbend, which announced to the disappointed pursuers that not only had Mullah Nour escaped, but that he was even surrounded by his comrades.

In Iskander's house the doors are closely shut. All is very quiet within; a faint whispering can scarcely be heard.

Gayety seeks the crowd; happiness loves silence and solitude.

Printed in the United States
208009BV00001B/52/A